THE HUNGRY COAST

The Hungry Coast

Fables from the North Shore of Minnesota

Stories by
Marlais Olmstead Brand

Woodcuts by
Noah Prinsen

NORTH STAR PRESS OF ST. CLOUD, INC.
St. Cloud, Minnesota

DEDICATION

"Sometimes I was so hungry, so very hungry,
and the hunger raged so in my veins that I was tempted,
O, how terribly was I tempted . . ."
~Angelique Mott

For my girls. As the song goes,
"Home is wherever I'm with you."

ISBN: 978-0-87839-819-5

This is a work of fiction. Names, characters, places, and incidents are the products of the author's imagination or are used fictitiously. Any resemblance to actual events or persons, living or dead, is entirely coincidental.

Printed in the United States of America.

Published by
North Star Press of St. Cloud, Inc.
Saint Cloud, Minnesota

www.northstarpress.com

TABLE OF CONTENTS

Timber Ghost

Louis Garoux   Madame Wiindigoo
The Old Road

Jet Black
White Fish
Great Gray

The Hungry Coast

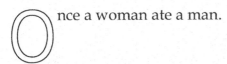

MADAME WIINDIGOO

Once a woman ate a man.

This was sometime in the middle of the 1800s, when copper was almost king. The North Shore was crawling with surveyors and prospectors. To start with, they were looking for silver. They heard Indians had a legend about silver and the men from the east listened. And their eyes got big as saucers with the prospect of the mother-lode and greed drove them up the shore, looking and looking.

They were up there in late summer one year, up around what is now known as Grand Portage. One fellow in particular, let's call him Smith, was poking around the Ojibwe summer en-campment, asking questions and generally making a nuisance of himself. Smith and his friend Small were from an eastern min-ing company which was looking to expand into new territory. Nobody paid these two white men much attention. The people had fish to catch and work to do before they pulled up stakes and headed inland. In those days, the Ojibwe wintered at what white men call, "Vermillion," up Mud Creek from Portage. The Ojibwe called the lake of the sunset glow Onamanii-zaaga'igan. Used to be that country up there was chock full of game. Back before the mining and lumber companies came, there were moose, deer, caribou, bear. Nobody went hungry then. But men like Small and Smith were already afoot in the interior. Soon there would be more of them and they would cut more and more of the woods away and they would dig into the bowels of the earth and tramp the old roads to mud with their beasts of burden. One day, whole sections of that country would be pocked with holes and studded with stumps. And one day, what game there was in the naked land would be shot to feed hungry jacks and mining men. The men from the east, loitering on the cobbles with their hands in their deep pockets, signaled that prospects for wintering in the interior looked bleaker by the day. Perhaps that's why Woman took another look at these white men with too much hair on their faces.

As she repaired her fishing nets, Woman listened. The men spoke bad Français, but she could understand much of the English. The tales of great snakes of silver slithering through the rock were nonsense, but her mind began to run along the shores, up the rivers and through the forests. The white men had things in their pockets that they offered for sweet maple sugar: beads, coins, crosses. Woman and her family were tired of such trinkets and knew that rarely was anything more than a trinket given. Most of the words that came out of such mouths were trinkets as well. But she watched her own hands weaving her net and she listened. A child rarely came to a hungry woman. The child quickening in her would need her to eat through the long winter. When the white man pulled his wallet from his vest, she saw that it was fat with more than trinkets. Notes enough to count many beaver. Notes enough for another cooking pot, and rations of the trader's salt pork and flour.

The next day, Woman went to the fishing grounds with her husband. They hauled in their nets and the fish were few. The mitigookamaig would be moving into deeper water now. The season had begun to turn. Woman looked down through the cold water to the stones far below. Time for change. Woman asked her husband if he thought the child would like the taste of fish. When he replied, "If the fish are here, the child will eat them," she made up her mind.

Back at camp, Woman went into her wiigiwaam. Carefully, she unwrapped a large birchbark packet. Inside, packed in pale green moss, was her luck and her wish. Fire caught in rock. It looked like a secret fish flashing in the dark. In early summer, she and her husband had made a camp on the Isle. There were many fish off the point. While hauling in the nets, she had spied her wish among the boulders below. She knew at once this would mean a child, and her husband had seemed to know as well. When she gasped and pointed, he stood and stripped, then dove into the lake like an arrow. He flew to the bottom. He rose up with his eyes open and bubbles streaming from his smile. His body was still cold like the stone many hours later. Miskwaabik was sacred. It was luck. It was a wish.

Without looking at her husband, Woman carried her wish to the white men. The smaller man saw it and knew it first. Then the taller one leaned forward and took it from her hands. His eyes were like moon medallions. She pointed out over the lake, to the Isle.

Notes were pulled from the fat wallet and placed in her hands. Her husband stood by her side when the deal was struck.

Later, in the bateau, she thought she felt the child move. But it was too soon. Only her imagination, her anticipation.

They floated over the point and copper flashed like fire below. It was greed that put Woman and Man ashore so hastily. In a few days time, they were told by the white pair, the bateau would return with provisions for the winter. Greed appointed them guardians of the copper at the bottom of the Lake. Greed put more notes in Woman's hands. The white men sailed away with the wish. Woman folded her notes into birchbark and buried them under a rock.

The first storm came the next day. Woman and Man believed this would delay the supply bateau and so they went in search of the remnants of their spring camp. They had cached a net and line, some plummets, a few hooks and some needles. They patched the old wiigiwaam by the shore and laid fresh zhingob boughs on the floor. When the storm cleared, they climbed a boulder and cast the net from the shore into a chasm of deeper water. They walked into the woods to find a suitable location for their winter camp. It took them a long time to decide, for Man was worried about the wind and weather on the Isle in winter. Woman told him that the men would return with a sturdy ax and Man grumbled that this was not the time for cutting saplings for a wiigiwaam. But, she said, there would be waabooyaan, blankets and kegs of salt pork. An iron skillet for the fire! Woman's eyes shone with the thought of that fire and fat crackling in the pan.

Days fell upon days. And still no bateau, no provisions. One day, the net got snagged on the bottom and man dove into the Lake to retrieve it. He shivered with cold for days, and the fish left as well.

The weather turned cold. Man began to cough and wheeze. Woman brewed mashkikiwaaboo and rubbed herbs on his chest, but he was hungry.

Man and Woman used a knife to saw through some saplings and they managed to erect a winter wiigiwaam in the woods, away from the beach. There were signs of Mooz there, but no good way to hunt them. Man began to make an arrow and a bow. He returned to the shore the next morning, thinking to check his net and use some line for the bow. When he tugged the line, it offered no resistance. The net was gone, perhaps pulled out in a gale during the night. The line was not right for the bow, so he made a crude snare and caught only two hares in as many weeks. Man and Woman were so hungry, Man turned the snare into a fishing line once more. The line was short and he had to fish in his own shadow. He lay on his belly on the big rock, dangling the line down into the water, so close to the surface, his wet hands would burn with cold and his fingers became sullen, like clay. The day he lost the second hook, they decided to move inland.

Days fell upon days and Woman and Man returned to the shore each day to build a fire. They searched the horizon for the bateau. Man began to have trouble with his body. He spat blood from his lungs. He was hungry and he began to be angry. The line in his pocket was not right for a bow, but he strung it anyway.

When the snow began, Man and Woman stopped making fires on the shore. Man was not strong enough to walk that distance, let alone track moose. Rabbits were scarce. One day, a bit of Woman's hair caught fire and filled the wiigiwaam with a scent like singed fur. Man rose from his pallet and grabbed Woman's wrist. He held her burnt hair to his face, drinking in the scent. Woman cried and struggled, and then Man cried too. He laid a hand across Woman's round belly and he cursed the brace of white men to death. Then he fled into the night.

Thinking of Man, Woman made a biskitenaagan and filled it with rabbit bones and water. She dropped a hot rock into the small birchbark bowl and as she watched the water come to boil, her tears salted the soup and the child twisted inside her. Man did not return that night. She found him at the shore, laying next to a fire he had built and never burned. His face was glazed with ice, and his eyes were open.

With much effort, Woman dragged Man into the old summer wiigiwaam. She laid a fire and lit it, thinking against her belly, against her life, that she would thaw her husband and he would return to her. The ice melted and ran like tears down his face, but his eyes simply stared.

She stayed with him until the fire died and then she walked back into the woods.

Sometime in the early morning of the next day, Woman awoke with one thought trapped in her throat: wolves. For some reason, she did not want Ma'iingan to take Man. No bateau, but a flotilla of wolves crossing the ice, following the scent of maazhise to fill their own taut bellies. What if Man returned and his body was gone? Nothing should take Man's body. Before it was light, Woman found her way to the shore and began to pile snow and branches around the wiigiwaam, making a cache of Man, hiding the scent of his body.

Days fell upon days. Snow fell upon snow. Woman spent her time trudging to and from her husband. She tied strands of her hair in the branches to warn away the wolves. She sang to her husband. She untied the string from the bow and used that to pull a few fish from the Lake. And then the Lake froze too thick to make a hole, and for many days she did not eat. Then she ate moss and bark from the azaadi. Then ashes. And when she ate ashes, she smeared her face with them in mourning and she called her husband. She fell asleep and Man came to her. He sat by the fire and smiled and bubbles streamed from his mouth. Then he held his arm over the fire and it began to crackle and sizzle. Woman awoke with the taste of salt pork on her tongue and she knew Wiindigoo was with her. She fled the lodge.

Outside, she found fresh tracks in the snow and followed them to the shore.

Sure enough, Wiindigoo had been circling her husband's wiigiwaam. But his tracks were not those of a wolf. He had come as a human and her own feet fit perfectly in his prints.

Woman grew very cold and she knelt down in the snow and called her husband to save her from Wiindigoo. But her words flew away in the north wind and suddenly a flame lit inside her. The flame grew to a fire of pain that devoured her and she called for death there in the snow and was answered in blood. After a long trial of anguish and pain, her child was no more.

Woman somehow returned to her wiigiwaam and made a fire, which she nursed for many days. And while she nursed the small smoking fire, she talked with her husband. He sat on the other side of the fire, and every so often he would begin to smile and she would beg him to stop, to keep his limbs out of the fire, to refrain from roasting himself. Woman knew Wiindigoo was with her. She knew Wiindigoo was the black ice in her belly, was her husband, was herself. When she thought of her husband's flesh, of his bones and of soup, she knew Wiindigoo. And so with great effort, Woman selected the strongest strands of her own hair and pulled them out of her own head. She wove a snare with which she caught a rabbit. And when she could not wait to clean the animal, her brother, and put him on the fire, and when she tore his raw flesh from the bone with her own teeth, she knew Wiindigoo was with her. After that first rabbit, she fought with herself to first cook his brothers and sisters before eating them.

Woman was still alive when the ice broke and freed the Shore. She was still alive when the snow retreated and left only her hair white. She was still alive when the fish returned and she caught a few in a basket of bark. And she was still alive when her husband began to thaw and the animals desired nothing more than to take his body. And so she was still alive, sleeping in the open, on the beach, guarding her husband, her wish and her luck, when the pair of white men returned. She woke to the sound of the bow of the bateau sliding over the cobbles on the beach.

When she stood, and as they laid eyes on her, Woman saw Wiindigoo reflected in their wide, white, fat faces. The small one stepped toward her and words began to fall out of his mouth. He bent over, stooping as if to pick up something he had dropped. He stopped making sounds and then the tall one came reeling up the beach. His blanched face began to flush, his nose began to leak. He stumbled and nearly fell. He was asking about Man. Three more came stepping from the boat. Woman saw that their hands were empty. The bateau was empty. They did not even bring the miskwaabik back to her. The short one wanted to know, Where was Man? She turned and gestured to the old summer wiigiwaam, piled high with boughs and branches. The tall one stepped to her. He began to weep. He said, "Madame, Madame, Madame." Three times, like a charm, and when he offered his hand to her, she accepted it. Wiindigoo's teeth quickly found his bone and tasted his warm blood in her mouth.

THE OLD ROAD

With special thanks to Staci Lola Drouillard and her project "Walking the Old Road"

There is an old cemetery in Beaver Bay. Looks abandoned. But it isn't. Not nearly. Mr. John Beargrease is buried there, as are his kin and countless others who made their way to the other place, so long ago, sometimes only the spirits remember them.

There are no good directions to the cemetery. You read something about the location, and then you guess. You can ask the locals where the place is, but most will pretend they don't know. They know all right, but they try to forget. They don't try consciously, the forgetting just happens, because it's easier. It is easier to forget the hunger of progress, the voracious devouring of the brothers and the sisters, the trees on the hills, the minerals in the earth, the animals in the woods, the fish in the Big Water. Much simpler to let ignorance wash over you like a clear, cold wave. Forget that people lived and died with the brothers and sisters and big, old Chigamig. Forget the time before Wiindigoo devoured them all whole.

But find the old sign, swinging beneath a tangle of low branches. Painted brown with yellow lettering, pointed like an arrow: INDIAN CEMETERY. Like an advertisement for tourists,

11

strangers who hardly ever come. The log stairs are rotting. The decayed handrail tempts you to grab hold and tumble down the hill. The place is haunted, of course. A few people know the place and love it for there is evidence of this. There are medicine bundles scattered along the narrow deer trail, dream catchers and some totems dangle in the trees and twist in the wind. The birch fall and bend in endless crosses, dividing the empty space into four corners. Old Gaag, Old Porcupine, sits and looks down over the mounds and the lone monument. There you will find a list of names in bronze. The plaque is fixed to stone and the stone is sinking into the earth. Soon it will meet the bone of bedrock below. Bone against bone, like the gnashing of teeth. Like a perpetual ice age, the scouring of rock with rock continues as time grinds forward.

It is guessed that some spirits are tethered to that old cemetery, committed to that ground, unable to pass away, over the river and on to the reunion of brothers and sisters. Stand at the top of that lonesome hill, survey the tangle of brush, the pickets of fallen birch, the names cast in English and bronze and hazard a guess: There was a crime committed and the dead cannot forget and so they cannot truly die. Instead, they cry into the wind and their lament is carried up and down the Shore. This lament, this cry, it is a warning, and when you hear it, take heed: When time uncoils and shoots like an arrow, instead of a wheel, Wiindigoo is afoot.

"Did you hear that?"

"What?" said Mr. Nelson.

"That sound," said his wife. "Like a sob."

"No," answered her husband, and he began to turn down the path to leave.

"There it is again," said Mrs. Nelson, quickly. Her voice was repressed, stifled but full of electricity. You wouldn't know it to look at her, but at that moment her hands were vibrating with a current she did not understand.

Mr. Nelson turned back and surveyed his wife of four decades and some odd years. "You're white. Like a ghost." And in the ensuing silence, just before he set off again, the wind sifted through the tree tops and something cried out.

It was one long keening that seemed to be up above or down below and over your shoulder and nowhere at all. A hot spike of electric fear thrummed up from Mr. Nelson's heart and straight through the top of his head.

There were no more words between them. Husband and wife stumbled down the path careful, even in their haste, not to grab for the rotting handrail.

When they reached the bottom of the stairs and blinked into the sunlight, Mrs. Nelson found she was gripping her husband's shirttail tight in her fist. Her knobbed knuckles were white. At their feet lay a track in the mud. Brother Moose had been there.

Old Mooz does not cry and keen, though. And the fact of the matter is that Mr. and Mrs. Nelson never even saw his track. Husband and wife got in the car and continued up the shore. Schroeder, Tofte, Lutsen, Cut Face Creek and down into Grand Marais they went in silence. They carried the silence between them like a large parcel they could not see around. Each contemplated the spruce, the basalt and Chigamig in isolation. Tree, rock and lake now seemed to have independence, personalities, minds of their own. If the wind could cry, why not a tree, a rock or the very water? They stopped for lunch and after Mr. Nelson had taken the first bite of trout, he said the first words to his wife after the silence, "Must have been the wind."

Mrs. Nelson stared at the fish before her. "Yes, it must have been."

After lunch, husband and wife did not stroll, but rather walked carefully along the harbor way. There was the lighthouse and the breakwater, but the things of man seemed flimsy rather than reassuring. As they approached Artist's Point, the wind began to pick up and they watched the Lake rear up over the volcanic rock with some trepidation. Intent seemed to uncoil in the waves and the whaleback of rock seemed sentient, like a great sleeping beast with infinite potential to awaken.

"We should get to the cottage," said Mrs. Nelson.

Her husband nodded and they turned their backs on the water and the rock.

Their destination was along the Croftville Road, but before they reached the turning, they were compelled to stop. There was a handsome church, on the right, just outside of town. But it wasn't the spare, simple beauty of the place that made them stop. You see, Mrs. Nelson clasped her hands together, as if in prayer. You wouldn't know it to look at her, but the gesture was completely involuntary and Mrs. Nelson felt as though a current was singing through her extremities. She was at a total loss. And at the very same moment, Mr. Nelson put his hand to his heart and this was a quick movement, very fast, but involuntary too. There was a great flash of pain in that heart, and the man cried out suddenly.

"Pull over!" exclaimed Mrs. Nelson.

And that is how they came to the old Chippewa Church.

"I'm fine," said Mr. Nelson in response to his wife's frightened eyes.

I am not, she thought, but did not say.

"Let's get some air," said Mr. Nelson as he stepped from the car.

"It's a pretty church," said Mrs. Nelson, following. She followed her husband around to the front of the church, which faced the lake. Now the view is crowded with trees, but once upon a time, the congregants could see right down to and out over the Lake.

"Doubt it's open," said Mr. Nelson, but he tried the front door anyway. It was indeed locked. For some reason, the Nelsons continued around the side of the church and they came upon another entrance and that door stood open.

Inside was a round woman seated at a desk humming a tune. She was certainly large, but she was short, too, and wore big, thick glasses which pressed into the brown flesh of her cheeks. Her dark hair was cropped close around her head. She wore a dark blue sweatshirt with an applique of a brown, be-ribboned, smiling teddy bear over her ample bosom. On her legs were light blue pants and on her feet were pink bedroom scuffs. She ran her finger over a line on a yellowed page in a sizable ledger and then carefully placed her pencil beneath the same line, as if marking the place.

"Martha Yellow Bells," she said. "That's what I thought." Then she looked up at Mr. and Mrs. Nelson through her thick glasses and smiled. "She married a Gasgon and sometimes the Gasgons called themselves the Gaskells and it's hard to keep track. They didn't care about those names the way we do nowadays. Didn't even always use their given names either. Too proud, too boasting. Like showing off. And half of them are across the road and the other half are down to the bay. It was that breakwater that did it. That an' the influenza and then the big fire. No influenza like that before the white folks showed up. An' then the depression, all that land bought up." The woman sighed and smoothed the yellowed paper with her plump brown hands. "You must be here to help then."

Mr. and Mrs. Nelson looked at each other. Mr. Nelson cleared his throat. "Well. It's nice to meet you. My wife and I just needed some fresh hair and then we saw the door open and—"

"Yes," smiled the woman. "I like to let that door stand open when I'm getting down to business. I'm not used to being cooped up in a church, even a pretty one like ours." And she gestured with her right hand in such a way that the Nelsons looked up and all around.

The room was bright and pleasant with yellow walls and white trim. The old wooden floor glowed in the sun, worn in such a pleasing way, making the passing of time seem so very gentle.

The woman stood with some effort. "I haven't even been in yet today. I should be airing it out too." And the woman opened a door into the church itself and the Nelsons followed her.

The walls were chinked log and also clad in boards of a very easy, refreshing blue. The woman stopped before the altar and ran a hand over the worn oak rail. The altar was dressed with fresh white linen and brass bits and bobs. "Never was one for church myself, but Daddy helped 'em build it and I guess I got a special place in my heart for it. Ma didn't like that Daddy did the work. She couldn't abide the nuns and such, but I suppose they needed the money and, as you can see, he was a real craftsman. Knew how to do it. Him and his brothers was the best around. Some did the breakwater too, of course. My dad was one. Did what he did in wood with stone. And breakwater's still there, right?"

The Nelsons nodded.

"It's very lovely," said Mrs. Nelson, beginning to walk down the center aisle. The pews were painted in a sort of soft tangerine color. A series of dark oil paintings hung on the walls, depicting stations of the cross perhaps. An old oak organ stood in the eastern corner by the door and a wrought iron gate served as an entranceway. There was a sturdy door in worn blue paint that led up to the tiny balcony and next to the door was a bellpull.

"Go ahead and pull it."

Mr. Nelson turned to look at the woman.

"The bell. Go ahead and ring it."

Mr. Nelson let the fingers of his right hand graze the coarse rope.

"They used to ring it right through the burials. Seemed like hours. Ma always had me help with the washing up after everyone ate. It's got a real nice sound."

Mr. Nelson gripped the thick rope in both hands, like a snake, and pulled down.

"You got to go at it good."

Up and down it went and the clapper struck the bell and Mr. Nelson's arms carried the sound that filled the air.

Then Mr. Nelson released the rope and the sound was gone and the air was empty, but for a shadow of that sound.

"Well," said Mrs. Nelson, her cheeks pinking up a bit.

The woman turned again. "Organ came back to us all the way from the Cities. Still works." She pushed up her glasses and looked at Mrs. Nelson. "Do you play?"

Mrs. Nelson blushed. "Just piano."

"You can get a tune out if it then. Go ahead," said the woman and Mrs. Nelson obediently sat down on the stool.

"Pump with your foot," encouraged Mr. Nelson.

The organ wheezed and sighed to life and one long note struck and faded like a cry. They watched Mrs. Nelson pull her hands into her lap and together they stared at the keys as silence returned.

"Glad you folks came along. I can sure use some help." The woman turned back down the aisle. As she shuffled away, the Nelsons looked at each other and shrugged.

Nevertheless, Mr. and Mrs. Nelson walked back out into the sacristy where they found the woman hastily closing the ledger and gathering a plastic bag of brightly colored knitting. "Forgot. Got to get my granddaughter from her swim lesson down at the campground. Sorry about the rush." She looked up at them briefly and squinted. "It's good you doing what you're doing. I'm so hungry for answers now, I could spit!" She laughed then. "All those names just getting lost to time. All that forgetting. An' Andy's done so much work across the street already. Soon we'll get the names up and, oh!" She looked at a watch that was not on her wrist. "I got to go. Sorry, folks." With that, she backed up a bit for them and the Nelsons crossed before her and out the door. They turned and watched her place an old key in the old black lock. When she looked up at them, together they said, "Thank you," and then the Nelsons turned and walked away from her, back to the car.

They did find the turn for the Croftville Road and they pulled into the small collection of cottages where they would find theirs, number seven. Before they got out of the car, Mrs. Nelson turned to her husband and said, "Where was her car?"

Mr. Nelson had the door open already, but he stopped and turned to his wife. "What?"

"That woman. Did she have a car? I didn't see it. She had to go get her granddaughter. How did she?"

Mr. Nelson thumbed his nose and then began to pull himself out of the seat. "Maybe she walked."

Mrs. Nelson said, "But there was only the highway," but her husband had already shut the door.

Husband and wife passed a peaceful afternoon by the Big Lake. They walked on the cobble beach and sat by the window, which

Mrs. Nelson propped open to hear the waves. They sat by that window and watched the water without words for quite some time. Eventually Mr. Nelson rose to stretch and find a sweater, for the night was bringing a chill with it and the window still stood open. Mrs. Nelson cast around the small sitting room a bit and leafed through a tidy stack of brochures and local newsletters stashed in a magazine rack. She sat again, turned on a light and began to read through a back issue of one newsletter. Mr. Nelson returned from the bedroom and began to work at packing his pipe. He whistled just a little while he tamped tobacco into the bowl.

"I'm sure you'll have to do that outside," said Mrs. Nelson, still reading.

Her husband looked at her, a familiar smile on his lips, about to return his wife's quiet rebuke with a small parry, but his eye fell on the newsletter she held in her hands, for there was a picture of the woman on the back page. The woman from the old church.

"Eleanor."

His wife looked up with feigned innocence, ready for the rejoinder about his pipe. "Tord."

He gestured with the pipe in his hand. "Did you see the back page?"

She shook her head, momentarily confused.

He jabbed the air with the pipe. "The back page of that thing."

His wife turned the newsletter over, scanning the image with her eyes. She swallowed, looked up at her husband with a helpless face and then her eyes returned to the page.

"Eleanor. You're white again."

She stood up and walked to her husband. She pointed at the picture of the woman. "She died last year."

Her husband made a sudden sound, a laugh that was more like a surprised bark. "No, can't be the same woman."

But there she was in her glasses. Even the same appliqued sweatshirt. Dottie Morton. She was smiling. The issue was dedicated to her, in memoriam, "for her tireless efforts to connect our people with our past." The old key to the old church was buried with her.

Tord and Eleanor returned to the Chippewa Church that very evening and found a shiny hardware store lock on the sacristy door. They returned to the cabin and Tord went looking for the cottage caretaker, looking for answers, but she was not in. Tord called the number listed on the newsletter. A prerecorded voice told him to leave a message, send an e-mail or visit the Historical Society for more information. In the morning, Tord and Eleanor went into town and waited in the harbor, watching the water and the birds, for one and a half hours until the Historical Society opened.

Inside the Historical Society, they found a woman who knew Dottie Morton very well. This woman was very close to their own age and quite friendly and talkative. Tord and Eleanor did not tell this woman about the woman in the church, but they asked many questions about the church itself and listened hungrily to the details of history at the foot of the Big Lake. There was a city, with people, land, a cemetery. Things had been lost and some found, but the old Chippewa Church was still standing, with tales to tell. But the church was all locked up these days, in need of someone to unlock the doors and air it out.

"Used to be open the last Sunday of every month," said the woman, "and whenever Dottie was in doing her research stuff, she aired it out." The woman sighed and ran a hand over her short white hair. "Not anymore." She looked at them with eyes as blue as a sled dog's. "Can't hardly get the grass cut these days."

When they felt they must surely go at last, Tord and Eleanor turned and headed for the door. When Tord's hand was on the brass doorknob of the former lightkeeper's house, the woman called to them, "Used to be a road along the shore there."

Tord and Eleanor turned back to the woman.

"The church faces the Lake. They could walk along the shore, all the way, right into town. Dottie always wanted to walk the old road. 'Wish I could walk the old road,' she'd say. I told her we should have a campaign, get permission from the folks with houses built right up to the water, do a walk. But she just shakes her head and smiles. 'Wish I could walk the old road,' she says, like that. *'The old road.'*"

The following year, right in the middle of a hard winter, Tord and Eleanor Nelson drove all the way up to Grand Marais, in a snow-storm no less, and bought a small cottage on the Croftville Road. The cottage sat back against the highway side hill and looked out across the road at a decrepit fish house that was leaning back into the Lake. There was a sign on a picket in front of the fish house and the Lake that said, "NO TRESPASSING" in unequivocal capitals. When Tord signed his name to the title for the cottage, he imagined a woman signing an X on a bill of sale for a piece of land once called "Margaret's Point." That summer, Tord and Eleanor joined the Historical Society in town and once a month they opened the old Chippewa Church for people passing by.

JET BLACK

girl was born in Norge. Her father died in Norge. Her mother died in Norge. When Onkel sold the farm, he took his niece across Atlanterhavet with him. When they reached the far shore, they traveled by rail, behind a svart locomotiv eating svart kull and billowing svart røyk, over the country until they finally arrived at the foot of the big Lake. A white ship called *America* took them up this Lake to their new home in America. Little Two Harbors was a small fishing camp of fewer than twenty-five folk. Mostly men, and two kvinner with a handful of children between them. All Norsk, but one. The girl, jenta, became a laundress, a stuepike, for fiskerne. And then she was a barnepike and a skole-laerer too, looking after and teaching the children.

The one who was not Norsk had skin the honey color of rav, like the pendant on the necklace of her mor. The girl once kept this amber pendant, like a golden tear, on a silver chain in the pocket of a svart kjole. Then she had only the one svart kjole, sewn by her mor when they buried dear Pappa beneath the rocky turf of her beautiful Kabelvaag. Her mor sewed a pocket into kjolen so that the girl might keep a small grainy picture of her handsome far tucked there, in a silver locket without a chain. The girl wore the svart kjole when she and Onkel set her mor beside Pappa, and she tucked Mor's rav pendant into the pocket, too. And she wore the svart kjole when they crossed the wide hav. And she wore the black dress when she stepped onto the dock in New

York. And she wore the black dress when she boarded the train because her mother's old painted trunk was stolen on the dock in New York. And she cursed the black dress with the twenty-one jet buttons down the back because her button hook was in the stolen trunk. She wore the black dress when they boarded the *America* and she hated the black dress when she had to ask a strange old woman who did not speak Norwegian for help. She could not ask her uncle to unbutton the black dress and the old woman's hands were so crippled with time that she could only manage five buttons. The girl stood, half-concealed in the lee of an open doorway, staring out at the naked cliffs of the strange Shore, while the old woman fought the dress, hissed in frustration and finally spat and shook her hands of the girl.

Within a few weeks of their landing at Little Two Harbors, a mother took pity and gave the girl a bolt of calico. The girl suspected the woman was also tired of assisting her with the twenty-one jet buttons. The girl sewed herself a dress, with shell buttons down the front and a pocket in the skirt. The work was not as fine as what her mother's hand had wrought, but it would do. The girl wrapped the black dress with the jet buttons in newspaper, placed it in the bottom of a fiskeboks and slid it under her narrow iron bed, but she did not forget it was there.

The one who was not Norsk, with skin like the warm amber pendant, had hair as black as the jet buttons on that dress. And his black eyes reflected the water when he looked out over the Lake.

The young man with black eyes also fished, like Onkel and the others. His smaller shack stood apart from the others, away from the shore, tucked into the trees, closer to the landing for the Light on the cliff. The girl learned that the young man spoke three languages: his own Indian language, which he called *Ojibwe-mowin*, Engelsk and her Norsk. He fished with a white-haired gammelmann in an open skiff. When the *America* docked at the landing for the lighthouse, the young man helped unload supplies and visited with the keeper who then gave him money, which she saw him put into his own deep pocket with his brown hands.

She watched the young man with black eyes. She did not know his name and was afraid to ask anyone, even Onkel. The young man played with the fishermen's children, throwing them into the air, chasing them over the cobbles and showing them how to fashion small nets with dried strands of nettle and aspen. She listened carefully to her young charges, but they never seemed to call him by name. In fair weather, he sat outside by a fire at night and carved rocks. When Onkel saw her watching, she looked away, but he told her that the Indianer was making weights for his nets. Onkel showed her the metal sinkers he used on his own nets and she understood that the young man had a method all his own. The young man and the old Norsk father left earlier in the morning than the other fisherman, and they usually returned to Little Two Harbors later than the other men. And the young man and the old father always had more boxes of fish to load on the *America* as well.

A year and a day after she and Onkel had arrived in Little Two Harbors, the girl hung a last piece of laundry on the line and walked to the edge of the Lake. The sun was lowering in the sky and the light was gold on the water. She watched the progress of the white skiff as the young man rowed across the west harbor to the fish house he shared with the old Nordmann. She watched the men winch the boat up the skids. She walked toward the house, wanting to see. She stepped down the narrow plank along the wall, carefully, over the water to the dock.

Inside, the young man was throwing fish out of the boat and the old man was standing with one foot on the bow, lighting his pipe.

"God ettermiddag," said the old father.

The young man looked up at the old man, who nodded in her direction and pointed with his pipe. The young man followed the pipe and found her in the frame of the door. His black eyes smiled and she saw his white teeth. "Good afternoon." He paused with a large whitefish in his brown arms.

She was suddenly embarrassed, awake to her strange boldness. "God ettermiddag."

He paused a moment longer with the fish.

Smoke issued from the old man.

"Kan jeg hjelpe deg?"

The old Nordmann began to laugh.

"Yes," said the young man and he suddenly tossed the fish, which she caught in her own arms.

"Hva er ditt navn, jente?"

She looked up from the wide staring eye of the fish in her arms and opened her own mouth, "Mari."

The old father laughed. "Mari!"

Mary was the name of the old father's wife. Mary Red Sky Drouillard. Mary Red Sky Drouillard became Mary Red Sky Nelson when she married Arvid, the Nordmann. Mary Red Sky Nelson was the mother of Gustavus Eagle Tree Nelson, the young fisherman with the amber skin.

Mari became Mari Eagle Tree Nelson and moved into the small shack in the trees. Mari learned how to mend and tend nets in new ways. She began to learn some English, and her husband's

Ojibwemowin as they cleaned, salted and smoked fisk, fish, *gii-goonh*. Her young husband began to cut and saw logs for an addition to their shack. Gus bought Mari more fabric and she sewed dresses for herself and shirts for her husband and his father, *Obaabaayan*, Arvid. During their first winter together, old Arvid died of influenza. In the spring, when the brutal, beautiful ice broke up, they placed Arvid under a *jibegamig* on a hill among the birches, and Mari began to fish with her husband.

The open Lake was so wide, she imagined Norse on the far shore. Imagined her far and mor on a strand, waving to her from a distance so great, she could not see them, but knew they were there. Mari's husband kissed her face and lips when they were out on the water, with no one to witness but the gulls overhead. She was loved in the sun and wind and so she loved these things nearly as much as she loved her young husband. Her husband taught her how to tie his plummets to their nets and she loved to watch the worn stones sink down through the clear water, dragging the nets down and down and down like nearly endless lines of laundry in the Lake, heavier with the water, pulled by a current moving below the boat, below everything, a strength made visible only by what it moved. *Guds hand*, she thought. It was like the feeling in her chest that she had for the man in her boat: she made the feeling visible. She was alive, there in the boat, because of the current that moved her.

And then came the storm in November, the day she stayed back, in the shack bundled and unbundled by turns, nursing her feber, at the mercy of her own small fire. And he rowed out and away and there was no one but his *Mishipeshu* to blame. The copper-tailed katt was a thief. She thought of the figure Gus had limned in charcoal one night by the fire. The beast curled on the face of the cobble, nearly dancing in the fire light. It was a thing from dreams with horns, and no wings. No wings. It tempted her to consider Martin Luther's djevelen. When he set his sights on the horizon, her husband offered his kobber katt gifts. He had whispers and tobacco for calm water. *Mishipeshu. Mishi-bizhiw.* His name sounded like the lash of his copper tail. And the day her husband rowed out alone, that tail whipped and mounted waves upon waves upon waves, driving the empty white skiff back to her cobble Shore. *Guds hand.*

She lay on the iron bed in her svart kjole and stared at the knots in the wooden rafters. She remembered thinking of the knots as eyes, the eyes of gulls, watching them there in the marriage bed as it rocked like their boat. She was never ashamed. But now they were just knots in the wood, places where limbs had been sawed off. The knots were scars in wood. Nothing more. And she was a woman in a bed alone, staring at the ceiling with a hollowness in her chest, and a stillness there, sealed from any stirring. Each of the twenty-one jet buttons were hooked. If she stopped breathing, it would be very quiet.

One of the Norske mothers came to see her, bearing a pot of suppe and a small loaf of black brød, but Mari was already gone.

The woman turned to see her crossing the harbor. Black in the white skiff. Mari's back was to the wind and her hair shone in the late sun. Her hair flew free in the cold November wind, *dakaanimad*, washing over her shoulders and around her face like so many copper snakes. The woman on the Shore had an impulse to cast the loaf out on the water, but the feeling passed and she turned away toward her own hearth, bearing the brød and suppe back to her own kith and kin before it cooled.

It was this same mother who laid Mari out on her own kitchen table when the men brought her back to shore. They were quiet, standing in long shadows cast by lantern light, wondering what to do with cold, wet, white Mari Eagle Tree Nelson.

But Mari wasn't there, she was still out on the water, beyond Ellingson.

Mari is in the skiff, adrift, facing Kabelvaag perhaps, but still adrift, giving up to the current. She knots her hair back away from her face. Cuts the net here and there. Ties the rope 'round her own black boots. She puts out just a bit of the first length of net, and she stands up in the *dakaanimad* to watch the beautiful stone plummets, his *asinaab*, sink, pulling the white rope down and down. Then she bends and fills her arms with net and stone and gives it all to the current. The skiff tips and, like an eye filling with a tear, spills Mari into *Chigamig*. Her svart kjole billows. She yearns for the flash of copper, the cloud of dark hair, the jet black eyes. She feels one tug and then another. She opens her mouth like a fish, to breath water. Again, and again. Mari is in the skiff, adrift, facing Kabelvaag perhaps, but still adrift, giving up to the current. She knots her hair back away from her face. Cuts the net here and there. Ties the rope 'round her own black boots . . .

WHITE FISH

Not so many years ago, a girl saw a ghost.

The day she saw it, she told her mother, "I think I saw a ghost."

Her mother did not laugh, but she did not exactly believe her either.

They were camping at Split Rock. They had the best spot in the whole place. Site number sixteen, if you must know. People covet that chunk of land, reserve the campsite a whole year in advance. Sits way up at the top of a cliff. Look north from sixteen and take care when you do, for the rail at the edge has seen better days and the drop is precipitous. But look north, and you are rewarded with a splendid view across Little Two Harbors out to the Light. A pretty, skinny tombolo separates the miniature harbors. Used to be a fishing village at Little Two Harbors. Norwegians in tarpaper shacks. Can't even see the pilings anymore. But that tombolo arcs out to a rocky island all covered with pointed firs. That island is Ellingson. And on the other side of Ellingson is as dangerous a stretch of Lake as you will find anywhere. But you look out there at Ellingson and you just itch to go exploring. And that is just what the girl wanted to do, get down there, cross that tombolo and put her feet on that old island.

It was just the two of them on that trip, mother and daughter. The mother was approaching middle age with fairly clear eyes, trained on her child, and the child was coming into young adulthood with a distant gaze, eyes fixed on any available horizon. The mother was hungry to know what was in her child's mind, who her daughter was becoming, and the girl could hardly wait to get out and down to that island, to stand on the rocks and face the water like a sea beyond. Can't see the far shore from Ellingson. Only the horizon. Lake could go on forever. But it was getting late and the tent had to be set up and a fire had to be started. While her mother was searching for a hammer, to drive the stakes, her daughter walked to the lichen-covered rail along that high cliff and looked down.

The wind was coming off the Lake and away down on the strand of the tombolo, a figure stood, facing into that stiff breeze. A black dress or coat whipped the wind. Man or woman? Hard to tell, but the figure was absolutely still, resolute, save the billowing black fabric. The very moment the figure seemed to turn, the mother called the girl.

"Come on and help me."

The girl said nothing of the figure, until later, when she remembered.

As the sun began to fade, after they cleared the dishes and tucked away the last of their fish supper, the mother and daughter made their way down to the tombolo. The wind had died and the sky was melting into the surface of the Lake. The horizon was invisible, just a gradient of lavender and peach. They walked over the cobbles and gazed into the clear, cold, still water. The mother wished for a fish. Wanted to see life dart through the clear water, and disappear. She wanted to know that the fish were there, hidden, but always there, swimming silver and growing fat and sweet-fleshed in the coldest, deepest water. The girl wished for something without a name, something bigger and sweeter than a fish, wider than the horizon. To the girl with the nameless thing swimming inside of her heart, Ellingson looked larger, more exciting by the minute. Just as the girl was about to scramble up the face of a boulder and leap on to the back of the island, her mother reached out to stop her. She pointed. A sign was posted and it forbade visitors to the island in order to preserve habitat. Then the girl wished for an ax to fell that sign. But the two turned away in silence, and before she reached the beach, the girl glanced back just in time to see someone disappearing behind the rocky point of Ellingson. What the girl saw was the back of a woman. A knot of copper hair. A black dress. Single row of jet buttons down the back. White hands clenched in fists.

"What is it?" said her mother.

"Nothing." But she wasn't nothing. She was something, and the daughter said nothing.

Later, mother and daughter sat by the fire, listening to the waves crash below them. The waves seemed louder and louder with each role, the surf gaining momentum and power. Curiously, the wind was slack, and a fog was creeping in. So stealthy was this fog, it was not noticed by either mother or daughter until it was quite thick and the leaves were dripping with moisture.

"What a fog," said the mother.

The girl had to use the outhouse.

"Take the flashlight," said the mother.

So her daughter took the flashlight and set out.

The light illuminated only a shaft of fog and the wall of night closed in around the girl. Branches and leaves disappeared. She had her own two feet and her noisy breathing for company. The sound of the Lake was gone. She was nearly there, crossing the little stream which ran through the culvert underfoot, and then she was there. With her own heart nearly strangling her, she reached out and swung open the outhouse door as fast as she could.

It was blessedly empty and she felt a wave of hot relief wash over her body as she placed the flashlight on the floor and prepared to do her business.

She sat. The silence was unnerving. Her water would not come. She took a deep breath and closed her eyes, focusing on relaxing and releasing her bladder. But what was that?

A sound. Something outside.

And then she lost control, despite herself, and she strained to hear the noises outside above the sound of her own urine.

Then all was quiet. The sweat was standing on her forehead, prickling in her armpits. She shivered and then froze.

There it was! A creeping, a rustling. A shuffling.

Dear God. She was going to die here. Eaten by a bear. Clawed to death. She cleared her throat loudly, began to bang about, hummed a ragged tune as she tidied up. And then, propelled by a surge of adrenaline in her blood, she burst out the door and barrelled straight ahead.

She ran as fast as she could down the narrow path. She had nearly reached the little stream, when she tripped and fell face first. The flashlight was knocked from her hand. She pushed herself up and looked for the light. Something moved off to the right. There in the beam was a swish of black hem, heel of a black boot and something white on the ground, trailing behind. A sound thrilled and thrummed in the stillness. And there were footsteps running, running. And there was her mother and the sound thrumming the stillness, parting the darkness, was coming out of the girl herself. It was a scream that did not end until her mother shook it out of her.

On the way back to the campsite, as the girl shook and sobbed, the mother met a worried neighboring camper and talked into his headlamp, explaining that all was well. Just a scare. Imagination. And the girl stopped crying, nodded and closed her eyes to the light. She went silent and waited. She let her mother hold her now, let her mother guide her down the path, one arm around her waist, the other training the light on their path.

She let her mother fold her into the tent and roll her into a sleeping bag and then she turned to her and said, "I think I saw a ghost." And then she told her mother about the figure in the distance, the wet hair the color of a new penny, the buttons, the boot, all that she had seen of the woman in black.

Her mother did not laugh. She nodded in the dark and then she held her daughter close. And when she held her child close, the scent of her hair, the damp softness of her feverish skin, these feelings brought the distant baby back to her, brought the tears of gratitude to her eyes. The mother patted her child on the shoulder, kissed her on the forehead and lay down beside her, but she did not sleep, not even when the girl finally let go of consciousness and drifted off.

When the first light came, the mother carefully and quietly unzipped the tent and stepped out into a damp and still early morning. She made her way down the path, listening to the birds tentatively flying from tree to tree. As she crossed the little stream, she looked down. There in the trickling water was a length of thin rope, like the stuff used for the old fishnets at the museum she and her daughter visited. She bent over to pick it up, but it was stuck to something upstream. She stepped down into the stream, balanced on a chunk of rhyolite, leaned over and tugged. Something small and heavy sailed up and hit her in the shoulder. It was attached to the end of the rope. It was a rock, but one that had been notched and carved to hold a circle of rope. An old sinker! What was the word? A plummet. That was it, *plummet*. She picked up the whole business and headed straight back to the campsite.

The tent was unzipped and flapping in a fresh breeze. The mother turned east, west, north and south. Her daughter was nowhere to be seen. A single path led to the campsite and the girl had not overtaken her mother. The waves were growing louder now, roaring as they rolled over the cobbles below. The mother stumbled to the weathered rail, laid her trembling left hand carefully on the old wood and looked over the edge. The waves rolled and curled over nothing but rock. She looked up and out to the north, and there was her daughter, making her way across the tombolo. The mother called her daughter's name, once, twice, but the waves rolled right over it. The plummet slipped from her right hand, bounced off a crop of rock and down, down it went, trailing the rope to disappear in the surf again without a sound. The mother turned and began to run down the path, over the stream. She didn't see the figure that now stood on that rocky point of the island. The copper-haired girl was dressed all in black, soaking wet, now beckoning to her daughter again and again and again, with a dripping, dead hand, white as the flesh of a deep water fish.

TIMBER GHOST

She was alive because she was hungry.

The morning the rest were killed, she was consumed by hunger.

"I'm going to go out and grab something. I'm so hungry."

"Now?" said Vince.

She had shrugged and smiled. "I'm just so hungry. Do you want anything?"

And he had said, "No. I'll wait. I'm in the middle of re-setting the Mimaki."

"Okay." That was the last thing she ever said to Vince.

Nobody else had wanted anything to eat either; it was too early.

"No, thanks. I'll hold off."

"Nah."

And, "No, thank you."

In fact, she had to wait more than fifteen minutes for the sandwich shop to open because it was so early. She had fretted, kept checking her watch, worried about taking too long. But her hunger kept her there, waiting on the sidewalk. And she had been licking salt from her fingers when the first police car whipped down the street. She had opened the bag of chips on her way back. She just couldn't wait. She was nearly done with them and suddenly there were more cars. And by the time she got to the corner, her head and neck felt strange. There were cop cars in the street and then cops crouched behind the open doors of cars, guns drawn. Incredibly, cops in bulletproof vests ran toward the shop. And then there were ambulances and more sirens and a cop stopped her with one big hairy arm like a board and she sank in slow motion down to the packed dirt and weeds beside the sidewalk, crushing the sandwich bag to her chest, while her mouth opened and nothing came out because everything was flying in. The truth of it had filled her up: something very terrible had happened and she knew it before she was told.

All five of them were killed. By the kid Vince's dad had not even really fired. Later, the TV said Randy had fired Darren. But he hadn't. She was there in the print room with Randy and Vince when Darren walked in, late for work with bloodshot eyes.

Darren had shuffled around, rubbing at a new tattoo on his bare arm. The skin there was greasy with something like vaseline. "Sorry, Randy. I overslept."

Randy kept on working the machine, peering over his cheaters at the proof. "Vince had to make the Peterson delivery, Darrey."

Darren sort of laughed, but didn't look at Vince standing there next to Randy. "Sorry, Vince."

Vince put his hands in his pockets and tried to look Darren in the eye. "Okay, Darren."

"Hey!" The three of them flinched because Darren was suddenly shouting, chin out, glaring at Vince. "I said I'm sorry, Vincent!"

Randy stepped from behind the bench and took his glasses off and approached Darren. "Those friends of yours are not friends. You can't come to work like this."

"Like what?" demanded Darren, clenching and unclench-
ing his fists.

Randy clapped a hand around the back of Darren's tense
neck in a fatherly way and shook him gently. "Aw, Darrey. Just
take a break for a while. Take a few weeks and get it together.
Get out of town. Visit your grandma. Get away from those kids.
I'll keep your job for you."

But Darren had twisted out of Randy's grasp and suddenly spun back on him, looming. "Fuck you, Randy." And then
he was out the door. And they were silent. And then Randy
shrugged and Vince shook his head. And she got hungry.

It was a family business and Darren had killed himself and the
entire family: Randy and Vince in the print room, Kim and her
twin, Kelly, in the front office and their younger sister, Nicole,
who they must have tried to hide under the big steel desk. And
nobody bought the business. Instead, it was all just divided up,
sold off and then the real estate sign went up. She noticed these
things from a distance. She was way back inside herself. A
cousin buried them all, beside Vince's mom, who was already
dead since Vince was a kid.

She was so far away, back inside, she didn't even go to
the funeral. There was just one for all five of them. Then again,
she didn't even know about the funeral until after it happened.
No one told her. All the people that knew her, knew about her
and of her, were dead. Her own parents were long gone. No sib-
lings. No friends anymore. The ones she had once were probably
in Milwaukee still, if they were anywhere. There had been Vince
and his family and now they were dead and she was alive to no
one, not even herself.

She left before the landlord told her she had to go. She had a yard sale in front of the apartment, just laid everything out on the small slope of lawn and sat there for a morning. Hardly anyone came. What day of the week had it been? She did not put prices on anything, just wrote FOR SALE on the flap of a cardboard box. A few people asked, "How much?" and it took all of her effort to say a number. She could not make change. Finally, she stood up and walked away with her sleeping bag and backpack.

The first week, she slept in Theodore Wirth Park. She wasn't scared. She wasn't anything at all. And still, it seemed any trouble would be very taxing and she was so tired, she was careful to hide herself away from strange people. She hated that she was so hungry. She despised the gnawing need inside her, compelling her to finally buy a sandwich or some other thing each day. She wanted only to recede and fade, but the insistence of hunger pulled her back up to the surface of things.

On the seventh day, someone caught her brushing her teeth in the restroom. It was a fit woman in cycling gear. She was polite. "Can I ask, do you need a place to stay?"

She could not look at the woman. Her voice had been full of concern. She just shook her head, turned on her heel and bolted out the door. Her heart was beating too fast. Someone had noticed.

Although it made her even hungrier, she walked all the way to the bus station. The bus went only as far as Duluth and by the time she got there, she was ravenous. She asked the driver about a truck stop and then she walked there.

While she ate, she looked around carefully. There was one woman at the counter. She listened to her conversation, then, determined that she, like the big sauntering, leaning and laughing men, was driving truck. She finished eating the greasy eggs and buttery toast, careful to scoop up the last wobble of strawberry jelly with her spoon. Six dollars and ninety-five cents worth. She could no longer stand the smell of coffee and instead drank a small glass of pulpless orange juice for one dollar and twenty-five cents. She left a tip of one dollar on the table and walked over to where the woman truck driver leaned on the counter, laughing.

She could tell the lady driver would be smoking if it was still allowed inside. Her laugh had an extra rasp and some heat in it. The driver was on the heavy side. An appliqued sweatshirt stretched over an ample bosom. Calico cats danced there nose to tail. The machine stitched script below declared, "My Grandma is the cat's meow." Her iron-gray hair was tightly permed and her rose-tinted glasses had rhinestones set in the bows.

She had committed to wait patiently for the driver to finish her conversation with the waitress and the man in the feed cap, but the waitress bobbed her chin in her direction before the talk came to its natural conclusion. The lady driver and feed cap man swivelled on their stools in order to appraise her, the interloper.

"You want something?" the driver asked skeptically, slowly crossing her arms over the cats.

She cleared her throat and met the squinting blue eyes. "I'm looking for a ride to Grand Marais."

"Oh, yeah?" Then the driver and the feed cap guy laughed. "This ain't the old days anymore, honey. We don't take hitchers." The driver held up a be-ringed index finger, long pink nail pointing vaguely over her right shoulder. "Sign says so."

She grew hot, knew she was turning red. There above the doorway was indeed a metal sign with a baked enamel finish which read, ABSOLUTELY NO SOLICITATION FOR TRANSPORTATION. THE MANAGEMENT.

"Sorry," she mumbled.

But the driver was laughing, saying, "Have to go find Bobby McGee, I guess."

She picked up her sleeping bag and backpack and walked out. It had begun to rain and she had forgotten to use the bathroom. She was too embarrassed to walk back into the truck stop. She and Vince had once been to Duluth. She had a vague idea that there was a big park north of downtown. Maybe the place was big enough to disappear overnight. She began to walk through the rain along a busy route full of shuddering and groaning trucks.

At a stoplight, she nearly fell off the curb when a horn blasted. Hydraulic brakes sighed and bucked. She turned to see a wall of semi, but the lady driver was up in the cab, behind the wheel. The passenger side window rolled down.

"Get in, then!" called the woman.

So she climbed up into the vibrating cab.

The driver said, "How much you got?"

She reached into her backpack and took out her wallet. She counted twenty-six dollars and forty-six cents.

The driver laughed and steered the rig onto a ramp. "Grand Marais ain't usually free." And as the truck turned onto 61, she added, "'cept for today. Today it's on special."

Larinda wouldn't take any money. And later, when they rolled down into Grand Marais and Larinda stopped at the turn for the municipal campground, she said, "If you're smart about it, you can find a spot up the hill in the woods. And the bathrooms are open twenty-four-seven, with hot showers." When she began to climb down from the cab, Larinda stopped her and poked her with a box of Lorna Doones. "Take this. My cholesterol is sky high anyways. And you got to eat. Eat, and then go find a job and get yourself to a doctor, girly-girl. You're going to need one."

Before she could say anything, Larinda reached over and pulled the heavy door shut.

Later, when she opened the box of cookies, she found a fifty-dollar bill tucked inside.

For six days, she camped in the woods and snuck into the campground bathroom late at night. She cut up through the wooded hill and over to the main drag when she walked down to town. She stayed out of the campground during the day.

There were other ragtag young people in town and nobody gave her strange looks when she asked for work. She was in disguise as another kid at loose ends. But the season was winding down, and nobody needed another waitress, dishwasher or cashier. "Try up the Trail. They'll be getting ready for winter soon." But there was no way to get up the Trail. She had no transportation, didn't want to ask for a ride, knew no one and didn't want to know anyone anyway.

On the seventh day in Grand Marais, she saw a sign in the window of the municipal liquor store.

"It's just part-time," said the manager. "Ten to four. And next month, I won't even need that. I might not have any hours for you next month." She took the job and that night she bought two smoked ciscos and washed her clothes at the laundromat.

It was colder that night. She bought a tarp at Joynes to keep her things more dry. She had been moving her site every night, to stay hidden, but on her tenth day in Grand Marais, she walked through the campground in broad daylight and registered in the office. Paying for the first week left her with only five dollars, but she would get her first check in as many days. As she signed her name to the registration card, the manager said, "At last you're legal." She forced herself to meet his eyes and and when she did, he winked.

It seemed impossible to be invisible.

"I got a used tent over there on the shelf." The manager pointed. "Pretty old. Full of patches. It's yours for ten bucks."

She looked at her hands and shook her head. "Thanks, but—"

"Pay me next week, then," he said and walked over to the shelf and pulled the tent down.

On her fifteenth day in Grand Marais, the bike appeared. There was a bike rack right outside of the liquor store and that is where the beat up black mountain bike appeared. Day after day, it remained. She checked on it before, during and after her shift. It was certainly forgotten.

On her nineteenth day in Grand Marais, she awoke to a heavy frost, thick as ice on the tent. It burned away in the September sunshine, but there was no mistaking the warning. And she was very cold at night now. She purchased extra socks and boiled cans of soup over her fire, but she stayed cold. And she stayed hungry. Every morning, she had taken to buying a bag of day-olds at World's Best Donuts. And she kept little hunks of cheese and granola bars in her pockets, but she was insatiable. Her hunger was so insistent, it woke her up at night and pulled her out of her dreams of Vince. She made up the dreams because she didn't sleep, not really and truly. True sleep was something from the time before. Now she shivered in her sleeping bag and conjured up a dream life.

In her dream, she and Vince were in town, on their honeymoon. They sailed the *Hjordis* in the moonlight and laid on the sun-warmed rocks out on Artist's Point. They ate big baskets of fish and chips at The Dockside and they drank wine and laughed on the roof of the Gunflint Tavern while the sun set over the Sawtooth Range. And, thanks to brochures she found in the tourist center, the dream went right up the Trail to a lodge for winter, where she and Vince snowshoed over the frozen lake, skied through the pine forest and lay in a warm bed by a crackling fire. The food, the drink, the heat, it was glorious. And Vince was alive. Vince's skin was warm to the touch and she existed. Down in Grand Marais, the big Lake was frozen solid.

On the nineteenth day, a tall guy with a ponytail, strong hands and paint under his nails walked in and bought a bottle of grape schnapps. "That your bike out there?"

And she looked right into his gray eyes as she handed over the change and said, "Yeah. That's my bike."

"Aw," he said, rubbing the back of his neck. "Interested in selling it?"

She shook her head.

"Okay. Well, I'm in the market for a bike. You know anybody with a bike, they can reach me at the Trout. I'm Frank." He smiled.

"Okay," she said and Frank left.

The next customers through the door changed everything. They were a picture of what could have been. They were the dream.

They were the right age. He was a little taller than the woman. They both had dark hair. The guy was lean, like Vince, with long ropey arms. They were clean and attractive, bright and rosy. Clearly on vacation, they could not stop touching each other. They giggled and lingered in the wine section, making fun of labels. In the end, they presented her with three bottles of champagne and a box of beer.

"You from here?" He grinned as he pulled his credit card from his wallet.

She shook her head. "Twin Cities."

"Oh, we are too!" exclaimed the woman, as if this was a magical coincidence.

"Got away from it all, huh?" continued the guy. "Wish we could do that. It's so amazing here." He turned to the woman. "Maybe we should do it." He grinned across at her again as he took back his card. His hands were strong and veined. His watch glinted silver against his tanned skin. "Should we? Do you just love it?"

She could not move her head in any direction. Not "Yes." Not "No." She could only look straight at them. But it did not matter, they didn't really see her.

He squeezed the woman and spoke into the hair at her temple, "Should we do it? Just have a permanent honeymoon? Huh?"

The woman laughed and gave him a playful shove. She turned and said, "Thank you," over her shoulder as her new husband pushed her out the door.

Mike was coming in for his shift and she nearly bumped into him. "Where you going?"

"Just a minute," she said, walking out the door. The couple were getting into a silver Toyota. They were laughing. She looked a the black bike in the rack.

She did go back into the liquor store and cash out, but when she was done, she pulled the bike from the rack. She walked the bike around. There was Broadway. She got on the bike, took a right onto 61 and the fifth left was the Gunflint.

Climbing up out of town was difficult. It was so steep, she had to rise up off the seat and throw her weight over the handle bars. She began to sweat. She had no water. Just her nearly empty backpack and her nearly empty wallet. But the wind was a relief and the sky was blazing blue. She looked back over her shoulder once, and then she let the water recede. Pretty soon, the Trail evened out and it got easier to keep going. Trees, ponds. A river. More trees. A swamp. Farther and farther away from the big, cold Lake.

People were right. It was amazing. The Lake, Grand Marais. Beautiful, she knew, understood it intellectually. But there was no way to feel the beauty, no way to get close enough to touch it. When she and Vince had stayed in Duluth, right before Christmas, they had eyeballed some brochures and talked about Grand Marais. "Maybe sometime we can go up and rent a little cabin," she said. They were sitting at the bar of a Mexican restaurant in Canal Park.

Vince had raised his glass. "Maybe sometime we'll have a good reason to do that," he said, draining his beer and then slamming the glass on the bartop theatrically and winking. "A damn good reason!"

For the rest of the weekend, she had replayed this exchange in her mind. Throughout the holidays a part of her anticipated something that never came to pass.

The Lake was big. So big, one had to imagine the size if you couldn't actually get out on it. The town was almost miniature by comparison. She felt as if she was peering into a doll's house. There was Artist's Point with its little pointed firs. The lighthouse. Loons. See the schooner with its red sails. Here is the fish house with its fish and gulls. It was the water that broke this illusion. The pellucid water was so cold that the coldness was a thing so real and immutable it could not be dismissed. It was nearly as cold as death, and certainly more real. The water compelled her to spend long minutes considering it, but the consistent, unremitting cold of it upset her deeply. She felt there and gone simultaneously.

Now she only felt compelled to pedal. The light began to fade and some part of her knew she should be worried, or at least concerned, about what might happen next. The miles were piling up behind her. Hunger would descend like night, but she couldn't feel a thing like that and was not driven to focus on these likely facts of the future. She was just driven to move right now.

She had passed signs for lakes and lodges, but hadn't considered them. Now she could see another in the distance, but she couldn't read it yet and the light was going. Suddenly, a crash up to her right. Something white burst from a stand of dark trees on the slope. She was trying to stop the bike and she saw a split hoof as she fell. Deer. The animal leapt clear and crashed into the woods to the left. She found herself under the black bike in the gravel on the shoulder of the road.

She stood up. The road was quiet. The bike seemed unharmed. Her jeans were open at the right knee and her knee was skinned and studded with tiny bits of gravel. She bent over and picked gravel out of the wound. Hers seemed to be the only sounds in a sea of silence. She got back on the bike and kept pedaling toward the sign.

Darkness was settling in at the edges of things and she could not read the sign until she was nearly on top of it: WAWASKESHI LODGE.

Lights glowed in the main building. Wind pushed through the tall white pines lining the drive. Beyond, a lake reflected the last light behind black trees that looked like paper cutouts. There were voices with laughter down there, the slosh of water and the knock of metal against wood. Likely a dock with boats and returning fisherman.

She walked the bike into the ring of light outside what looked like the main building and leaned it against the log wall, to the right of the entrance. When she cautiously opened the screen door, she entered a large and pleasant log-lined room with a dining area, a bar, rustic easy chairs, a few tables and low lamps. The room was empty except for one woman at the far end, dropping a bundle of firewood onto the hearth of a large stone fireplace. Without looking, she said, "Dinner service starts in a half-hour." Then she straightened up and turned.

She was tall and lean, with silver-streaked hair knotted up on her head and secured with red chopsticks. She wore faded jeans, a flannel shirt and work boots. When she pushed stray hairs off her forehead, the silver bracelets at her wrist chimed. Her eyes suddenly narrowed.

She tried a greeting, "Hi—"

But the woman cut her off. "What the hell happened to you?"

She followed the woman's gaze and looked down at herself. The knee was now trickling blood and had stained her jeans to the ankle. Her hands were very dirty and the heel of her palms were skinned as well.

The woman crossed the room and took her elbow. "You've got a cut on your forehead, too." Her grip was firm and she steered her into the nearest chair. "You better just sit down for a minute." She walked over to a table bearing a large crock with a spigot and filled a glass with water. "Weren't in a car, were you?"

She shook her head.

"Bike? Where is it?"

"Outside."

The woman handed her the water. "Helmets are a good idea."

The water was pleasantly cool and she drained the glass quickly. She was given another.

The tall woman watched silently with arms crossed as she drained the second glass. Her skin was tanned and her jawline was very square, almost severe. She took back the empty glass and said, "My name's Gene. What's yours?"

"Mary."

"Where you staying, Mary?"

It was then that Mary began to cry. The first tears rolled down and dripped onto her dirty, raw hands. She began to sob. The sobs gripped and wracked her. They moved through Mary in wave after wave. When she leaned forward, she cradled her abdomen and knew without a doubt why she did so.

That first night, Wawaskeshi Lodge was booked solid, but Gene put Mary up in the old Slabside cabin. Slabside had no plumbing or heating. It was one of the original cabins on the place and it had survived fires big and small. Nowadays it only hosted the odd old friend who happened to stay late or the occasional stranded fisherman. Mary was installed in Slabside that first night with a BLT and a space heater. Gene ran an extension cord under Slabside's only windowsill, across the lawn and into a plug in the back of the lodge, right outside the kitchen door. Mary got out her wallet, but Gene held up a hand. "We'll settle up later, Mary."

Late into that first night, Mary woke up to a persistent sound. At first, she thought she was dreaming, but it continued as she emerged into wakefulness. A scraping on the cabin door, strong enough to rattle the hinges a bit.

Mary sat up. *Scrape, scrape. Scrape.* She got out of bed. *Scrape, scrape, scrape.* It was insistent. Mary slowly crossed the floor. Cold seeped through the thick socks Gene had given her. Then it was quiet. Then there was a snort and a sort of chuffing. She shivered. A bear?

"Hello?" she said tentatively.

Scrape, scrape, scrape was the response.

She tiptoed to the window, but all she could see was the lawn and trees between Slabside and the kitchen. Whatever it was was out of sight.

The scraping became even more insistent. She should be afraid of a bear, but she moved forward anyway. She reached for the latch and pushed the door open a few inches. There was a snort and a clatter on the small granite stoop and when Mary peered out, she opened the door wide.

The deer turned and stood stock still, staring at Mary. It was white. By the light from the kitchen she could see that the doe—it must be a doe—was pure white, with dark eyes like holes in the white face. The doe bobbed her head. She snorted and turned and pawed the ground.

Mary stepped out onto the stoop. She was wearing a pair of Gene's long johns, and those thick wool socks, but she shivered in the cold. The doe tossed her head and pawed the ground again.

Mary stepped back into the cabin and looked around for the plate. There was only a small crust of bread and a few crumbs, but she walked back outside with it. The doe was nowhere to be seen, but Mary set the plate out in the damp grass, walked back into the cabin and shut the door.

Gene's cook decided to go to art school at the last minute, so Mary began by helping out in the kitchen. She washed dishes, set tables, ran food to the dining room and poured beer and wine. When the leaves turned, and it got busy, Mary began to get up early to make the coffee and set out the muffins. Then, after dinner dishes were done, she began to mix up the batter for the morning muffins and bake them while Gene tallied tabs. And one day, when Gene had to make an emergency run to town, Mary cooked cornbread, made salad, finished the chili and served lunch on her own. The next time cornbread was called for, she added cheese and jalapenos to the batch and a man from Saint Paul said he wanted to post her recipe on his blog. Little by little, Mary cooked more and more.

The kitchen was warm and the smells were reminiscent of a childhood she couldn't exactly recall. She enjoyed taking care of the fruits and vegetables, washing and slicing and organizing them into containers with tight lids and stacking them in the old walk-in. Little by little, she began to rearrange the kitchen. She made a new pot rack with old railroad spikes and lumber. She found a pickle crock in the back shed and then all the spoons and ladles had one spot. One morning, while Gene was fixing plumbing in number four, she made her own butter with fresh cream and added cinnamon and orange zest when she baked gingerbread muffins. The work made her tired, and hungry and alive. And each night, in a secret and strange token of gratitude, she left a plate of kitchen scraps out under the balsams by Slabside. She did not see the white doe, but she waited for her.

Two weeks in, Gene walked into the kitchen with a woman about Mary's age. She said, "Mary, this is Jenny."

Mary stopped stirring the wild rice soup and dried her hands on her apron. She offered the girl her hand.

"Jenny is guiding over to Bill and Carol's, for deer season, and then she's going to groom trails for Bev and Bob. And she's also agreed to wash our dishes too, at least the supper dishes."

Mary felt dizzy and suddenly wanted to sit down. Nothing good could last. That was the lesson.

Gene held out a piece of paper. "If you're going to be our cook, I figure you'll need some backup." The piece of paper was a personal check, made out to Mary. "You'll have to fill in your last name. Next check will be a real payroll check, if you tell me your last name. And I suppose you'll want to negotiate a bit of a raise, and maybe some time off. We usually slow down just before Christmas. That's a good time to take a breather."

But Mary didn't want to take any time off, even as she grew bigger, and more tired. Even her brief but intense morning sickness didn't keep her from the kitchen. Instead, she ordered up fresh and candied ginger and ginger tea and worked with the windows open. She made Thai ginger soup, more gingerbread muffins, and gingerbread cookies and three kinds of curry.

The first time Mary drove the old Ford into town for supplies, she stopped at Buck's. With some of the money from her first paycheck, Mary bought a fifty-pound bag of corn. When Gus loaded it in the back for her, he winked. "Gene ain't baiting deer now, is she?"

Mary blushed. "No. It's not hers. It's for me."

Gus stopped and looked at her. "You know you can't cook with this corn, right? You're doing the cooking up at Gene's, ain't you?"

Mary nodded. "Yes, I am."

He shook his head. "Well, this ain't food grade, technically."

"Don't worry."

"Oh, I won't. But don't you expect me to eat that famous cornbread of yours anytime soon!"

When Gene helped Mary unload the supplies, she only said, "Where's the corn going?"

Mary blushed again. "My cabin." Then she added, "I used my own money."

As Gene rolled the sack into the wheelbarrow, she said, "I never doubted that."

Mary still saved a few kitchen scraps, but now she added a handful of corn.

When the first snow began to fall, Gene came into the kitchen and said, "Time to move, Mary."

Mary stopped what she was doing and swallowed.

"You've got that look again." Gene took off her work gloves and laughed. "Listen, I just mean little Slabside is too cold for the weather that's coming down the pike."

Mary swallowed again, but kept stirring her potato soup. "No, it's not. It's fine."

"Fine if it had insulation and real heat, but it's run its course this season. Besides, I usually start using it to store the boat gear and stuff that can freeze. Number Four still has some plumbing issues, but at least it has plumbing and some insulation. I think we ought to move you over there."

"What about the bookings?"

"Oh, I've held off on booking Four. That's where the cook bunked last winter."

Mary stared into the pot. "I'd rather stay in Slabside, Gene. Go ahead and book Four."

Gene sighed and left for the dining room.

That night, as dinner was being cleaned up, Gene handed Mary a cup of tea. "Sit down for a minute and drink this."

Mary took the cup, but did not sit down on the kitchen's lone stool, so Gene did.

"Phil will be here tomorrow to get to work, but you'll have to sleep in Four for a couple of nights, okay?"

"What do you mean?"

"He's going to put in a Therma Tru and nail up some insulation. Nothing fancy, and no plumbing. You'll have to keep using the shower in the bunkhouse. And we don't have a storm for that old door, but I've got one for the window."

Mary smiled. She tried to stop her lip from trembling.

"Got to keep the cook happy, right?" Gene patted Mary on the shoulder and stood up. "You better buy some boots next time you go into town. Something with traction. I fell hard when I was pregnant and busted my tailbone. Very painful."

Mary had no idea that Gene had children, and before she could say anything, or even look at her, Gene was gone, swinging out the back door, into the snow.

That night, Mary moved her things into Four and slept there. Phil would be on the place early. In the morning, a light blanket of snow covered everything. Mary rose in the dark and headed out. It was hushed and snow drifted down from a bough in a light breeze. No doubt sunshine would later melt it all. The air was cold, but not frigid. Mary was heading for the kitchen, but she stopped to collect the leftover plate at Slabside. There were deer tracks in the snow. And all the corn, and the leftovers were gone. "Hello," whispered Mary. She couldn't help smiling.

Winter came and kept coming. Mary cooked and grew. On New Year's Day, late in the evening, Mary and Gene sat resting by the fireplace in the empty dining room.

"When is your next doctor's appointment?" asked Gene.

"Wednesday."

"Coming right up." Gene took a sip of her scotch and continued. "The weather can be iffy up here come April. You've got to consider your options. Mellie G., over on Poplar, was a registered nurse, a midwife for a time too."

"What options?"

"Well, you could go down to town for April. They told me to do that. Kristy and Mandy would probably have a spot at the B&B. You could do some light cooking for them."

"So that's what you did?"

Gene shook her head slowly, staring into the fire. "Nope. That is not what I did."

Mary suddenly felt cold.

"I was up here. Richard called Mellie. She was a registered nurse then."

Mary looked down into her mug of tea. "What happened?"

"Oh," Gene sat up straight, drained the scotch and stretched, "I delivered Henry right in Number Five."

Mary looked up and Gene met her eye with a smile. "He arrived very quickly, despite my broken tailbone. Just rammed his way out." Gene settled back in the chair and her gaze returned to the fire. "Of course, I couldn't really walk for a while and it still hurts sometimes when the weather gets wet."

They were quiet.

"So Mellie still lives over on Poplar and she was a practicing midwife for years after she delivered Henry. I gave her a call. She'll be around in April. No travel plans. She's a die hard, hardly ever goes anyplace warm."

"Thanks, Gene. I'd rather not go to town."

"Oh, we'll try to get you to the hospital of course. But it's nice to have a back-up."

Mary was surprised to realize that she had never before considered a back-up for the birth. She had not been looking ahead, precisely. She had certainly been taking care, and considering her baby, but she had not been looking ahead specifically. The future was, well, it was the future. "Thanks again for putting me on the insurance."

"Richard and I always ran the place that way, since our first full-time employee who was a guide, and a cook. Good guide. Bad cook. But that was before people really fussed about food up here."

Mary did not think she could ask the question she wanted to ask and so they sat in silence again.

Then Gene said, "Richard and Henry were killed on 61. They were coming back from the airport in February, after visiting Richard's mother. A southbound truck lost control on the south side of the Silver Creek tunnel. Crossed the center line. Henry was five, going on six."

"Oh, my God." Mary held her breath.

"I drove down once. To see. But I haven't been back since. Never go south of Castle Danger, actually, if you can believe it."

Mary nodded and tried not to spill the tears in her eyes.

"He's dead, isn't he?" said Gene.

Mary swiped quickly at her eyes. "Yes."

"How?"

"Vince and his family were all shot." The words were like cold marbles in her mouth. "To death."

Gene nodded. "In the Cities. I read about that."

They were quiet again.

"Just keep moving forward, Mary. This is a good place for that."

Mary went through more than three hundred pounds of corn that winter. She did not see the white doe until February.

She got up at three in the morning, knowing why she couldn't sleep. She could tell that the previous day was the anniversary of the accident, because Gene hadn't spoken all that day and her eyes were rimmed red. Gene did not show up for dinner either, and Mary asked Jenny to take a sandwich to Gene's cabin after the evening service. But Jenny came back with the entire sandwich and a half-empty bottle of scotch. Jenny put the scotch behind the bar and Mary put the sandwich away in a container in the fridge. Sealing up that sandwich and storing it uneaten in the cold was a sorrowful thing. And Mary felt cold and at loose ends for the rest of the evening. So at three, when she got out of bed, she had given up on sleep. She opened the door, thinking she would like to look at the moon, which was full. And there, practically on the stoop, was the white doe. She snorted and pawed the ground.

"Hello," whispered Mary.

The doe lowered and raised her head and then, to Mary's surprise, stepped forward. She walked to within a foot of Mary. It was clear that the doe was pregnant. Her belly was large. Without thinking, Mary stepped to one side and the doe walked right through the open door into Slabside. Mary wanted to shriek with delight. She leaned forward and peeked in. The doe had nosed open the sack of corn by the door and was helping herself.

Mary was afraid to go in after the doe and before she could decide what to do, the doe stepped carefully out over the threshold and the granite slab. Mary let her hand brush the animal's back and flank and the doe leapt away and was gone in an instant.

Mary's heart thrummed in her ears and suddenly her own baby kicked. "I'm your mama," she whispered.

The next night, and every night thereafter, Mary would double the portion of corn she left for the doe.

In March, Mary was so big, it was tricky for anyone else to be in the kitchen with her, but she kept cooking. She hummed while she cooked, enjoying the busyness, and the way her kitchen fit around her. From time to time, bits of Vince drifted into her mind and she stopped humming. His sunglasses. His knuckles. The hair on his wrist. Bits and pieces that did not hold together. It was as if Vince was dissolving, flying away, scattering to a far corner she could not see, around the curve of the earth.

She did not want to know the sex of the baby. It seemed like too much to ask. Too definite. She was big now, bursting with life in her kitchen and asking for more just now seemed greedy, and dangerous. When she tried to summon something of the way the child might look, her stomach felt like it was falling away. Then she would turn to her work and keep humming.

Late in March, Mary had a terrible dream. The white doe was pawing at the door. But Mary was bound by something and the doe pawed and pawed in desperation. When Mary finally threw off the unseen weight, she blindly circled the interior of the cabin, feeling for the iron latch with desperate hands like hooves. She could not see or feel her way to the doe. When at last Mary opened her eyes, she swung out of bed and ran to the door. She wrenched it open and, as the frigid air hit her lungs, she realized she was awake. In the early light, she could see hoof prints in the snow, and dark spots. She turned on the light. Blood. A trail of blood led away from her doorstep. Without thinking, Mary stepped out into the snow in her stocking feet. She registered a shock of cold, and then her water broke.

Mary wanted to follow the blood trail, even as Gene pushed her into the truck. She tried to explain about the doe. "Pregnant doe. Got it," said Gene. "I'll look when I get back."

But then Mary tried to shove her aside and Gene swore, "God damn it, Mary!"

That shocked Mary into stillness for a moment, and then she burst into tears.

"Okay," said Gene. "I'm going to call Jenny right now. She'll have to come over and get things started for the morning and hold down the fort. Jenny will check it out for you."

But even as they sailed down to town, the contractions coming harder and faster, Mary worried about the doe. She imagined wolves and ravens. Carnage in white snow, the doe torn asunder and scattered to the ends of the forest. She could not stop the tears that came. The towel beneath her was soaked. She was sweating and crying and leaking. Her entire body was weeping.

Gene said, "Keep breathing, Mary."

When the dark-haired boy was finally born, he was as pale as snow. And then he turned blue and the doctor and the nurse seemed to multiply and soon the room was full of people and then the dark-haired boy was gone. The doctor said, "Too much blood." An I.V. went into Mary's arm and Gene appeared overhead.

It seemed like days later that she woke up, but it was only a few moments. And then they wheeled Mary into a room and pushed and pulled her gently this way and that, swabbing and blotting and changing things and she was so very tired, beyond tired. Tired enough to be dead and not care in the least and then she slept like death. And when she awoke, it was Gene with the nurse. Gene saying: "He's out of the woods, Mary. We'll go see him now."

They put Mary into a wheelchair and wheeled her out of the room and down a bright hall and she thought of a morgue and steel tables and then they were in another room and there he was on his back, in a plastic box, with a tube in his nose and he was not pink, he was too white with hair the color of Vince's hair. And the nurse put her hand on Mary's shoulder and she said, "Soon you'll be able to hold him, honey." And Mary felt as if the life had been pulled from her, as if someone had simply jerked out the plug and her spark was gone.

She began to cry and to repeat, "I can't. I can't do it. I can't." And they wheeled her away from the baby in the box.

Gene carried the boy from the hospital, to the car and then into the lodge for the first time. Mary simply followed Gene through the back door, into the warm kitchen.

Jenny was at the stove, stirring soup, and when she turned to them she grinned, clutched Mary's arm and in an excited whisper, she said, "God, Mary! Look at him!" The tiny sleeping boy in his car seat was set down on the steel work table.

Mary felt rather than saw the look that passed between Gene and Jenny.

"He's still waiting for a name," said Gene. Then she turned to Mary. "I think Jenny's got something for you."

Jenny wiped her hands on her apron and hustled back to the far corner of the kitchen, between the stove and the wall. She gestured down and then put her hands on her hips. "It's been touch and go, but I think she's going to make it."

Mary saw that a cord snaked over a shelf and was duct taped to the wall in the corner.

"Warmest spot is right here, I figured. I figure she's a girl. But who knows. Soon she'll outgrow the cardboard box, but as long as the inspector stays away for a while, we should be okay."

Gene gave Mary a nudge and so Mary rounded the work table to see what Jenny was looking at. On the floor, in a box with a towel, under a heat lamp was an impossibly small fawn curled up nose to tail. It was as white as snow, but with light brown patches here and there.

"Sleeping like a baby." said Jenny. "After she has her bottle, she just konks out for an hour. Nothing wakes her up, not even pots and pans banging around."

Mary knelt down before the box. Enormous ears. Nose like a black button. White hairs so fine, so perfect.

"She'll be up soon enough, meowing like a kitten for more," added Jenny. "She can walk, you know. Tap, taps right around the kitchen like a little princess."

Mary thought of the blood and the doe.

Jenny crossed her arms. "She thinks she's a person, of course."

Mary sat on the floor in the ensuing silence.

Gene cleared her throat. "Jenny said she was curled up near the doe. Already half-frozen when she found her. Out under the big white pine by the dock. Far as I can tell, she was way too early."

Jenny continued, "But the heat from the doe's body must have saved her. She was still warm when I found them."

Mary stared at the sleeping fawn. "What happened to the doe?"

It was quiet before Gene spoke. "She's in the lake, Mary. I like the wolves to get their due, but I had a feeling this time that would bother you. I asked Phil to cut a hole out in the middle. Ground's frozen solid, of course. So she got her burial at sea."

Before Mary could say anything, a long cry pierced the air and the fawn jumped from her sleep, scrambling over and around Mary in a frantic jumble of legs and hooves. The boy was awake now.

Mary rose. The fawn skipped and slipped over the linoleum while the boy arched and cried. Gene unbuckled him from his car seat and handed him to Mary.

He was vibrating with life, angry and red with the desire to be fed. He was warm and wiry. His fist clenched around Mary's finger. Mary walked through the kitchen door and crossed the empty dining room. She took the rocker before the fire and then began to feed her son.

Presently, the fawn appeared at Mary's knee and began to nibble at her pants. Then the kitchen door opened and Gene crossed the floor and gazed out at the thawing lake. There was one place out in the middle where a thin ridge of snow framed an iced-over hole.

"I'm going to call him Henry, Gene. If that's all right with you," said Mary.

It was quiet and then Gene came and sat in the armchair. "That's all right with me."

Mary and Henry and the fawn called Patches slept and ate in Slabside. Then March turned to April and Mary began to cook again, with Henry and the tiny fawn there in her kitchen. Jenny and Gene helped out and the season slowed down until they were just cooking for themselves. Jenny left, with plans to return for the summer season, and Gene began to swap snowshoes for fishing gear, getting ready for the early sports coming up the Trail.

Patches grew up and one day she went into the forest and did not return for a month. From then on, Patches visited Mary and Henry, but she no longer lived with them. And then one night, Patches pawed at the door of Slabside and when Mary opened the door, with Henry on her hip, the doe walked right in and presented her own fawn, who was brown with white patches, like other fawns. The next day, a tall man on a bike stopped at the Lodge for lunch. He had familiar gray eyes and a ponytail and paint under his fingernails. His name was Frank and he was a boatbuilder in Grand Marais. After that, when Frank wasn't working, he came up the Trail, in his truck, to visit Mary and Henry. When Mary went into town for supplies, she stopped by Frank's boatworks down at the harbor. Henry tried to swallow sun-warmed stones while his mother talked to Frank. Frank fished the stones out of Henry's mouth and kept talking.

Over the next few years, Patches visited the lodge from time to time, but they never saw her fawn again. On Henry's third birthday, Gene offered Mary part interest in the lodge. Mary shook her head and smiled. "Not yet, Gene. I'm going to spend this summer in town." Frank and Mary married. They spent that summer in town and then Frank built canoes at the Lodge the following summer. One night, while they slept in Slabside, they were awoken by pawing at the door. Frank opened the door to thin air. Mary walked out into the moonlit night, but there was no sign of

Patches. Just as she turned back to the cabin, she heard something and turned to see a white deer bound down the hill. Thinking she must be dreaming, Mary followed. She stopped at the bend in the path. The white deer stood beneath the tall white pine, down by the dock. Mary held her breath. And then it was gone and Mary could not explain how it had gone. The next morning, Frank left for town, but he came back too soon. Patches was in the back of his truck, hit by a car on the Trail, just south of the Lodge.

When Henry was four, Mary gave birth to his sister, Frankie. Soon Henry would go to school and so Mary and Frank made plans to live in town in winter and return to the Lodge in summer. Gene also asked Mary to return to the Lodge on holidays and during busy weekends to cook for guests who had come to expect Mary's cooking. Mary began to work on a cookbook of Lodge recipes that fall and the family returned to the lodge for the winter holidays. Frank drove down to town to visit his parents on New Year's Day and stayed the night. Mary stayed on at Slabside and slept in their bed with the baby, but something woke her. She knew she had imagined the familiar pawing, but she headed for the door anyway. When she opened it, she was bludgeoned by the air as if it were a solid thing. There stood the white deer. It gazed at Mary with dark eyes. Mary held out her hand. When the deer pawed at the snow, there was no sound. The snow was blank.

Henry came to his mother's side, rubbing his eyes. "Is it her?" he whispered.

Mary looked down at her son. "Who?"

"The mama in the lake."

Mary felt a shock like electricity and her body seemed to resonate.

Together, they turned to the doe, but she was not there.

The next day, Frank's car was struck by a runaway logging truck on the Trail. His pickup was just climbing the steep hill above town when the logger lost control on the ice and crossed the center line. When the police arrived at the Lodge on the second day of the new year, they told Mary that her husband was killed on impact.

Mary did not go back down to town that winter. But bottles of scotch sat on the shelves untouched and Jenny did not have to stay on to help very long at all. Mary cooked and cooked and Gene and Mary took turns taking care of Henry and little Frankie. For a while it was hard to eat, but easy to cook, and cook, whether there were guests or not. It was a very long winter, as long and as icy as a tunnel that they had no choice but to slide down, slowly, with little control. In spring, Mary began going back down to town and Gene had the lawyer write up papers and Mary signed them, officially taking interest in the Lodge. Mary understood that Gene was likely the most generous person she would ever know and she also understood that there were no words to encompass this knowledge. Only hard work and loyalty could begin to account for her side of the deal in this life. The kids took the long bus ride up and down the Trail to school in town. They grew up and went to college and came back in the summers to work at the Lodge. Once, when Henry brought his fiancée back to Wawaskeshi for the holidays, he sat up late with his mother.

Henry stared into the fire and then he said, "Mom, why did you keep living in Slabside? Weren't you afraid of seeing her again?"

Mary turned and looked at her son, "I was never afraid of that white deer, never will be. She saved my life."

"What about Patches, and Dad?"

Mary looked into the fire for some time and then she took a very deep breath and let it out slowly. "She isn't an omen, Henry. She's just a messenger."

LOUIS GAROUX

There was a boy who cried like a wolf because he was a wolf.

Not so long ago, a mother witnessed something she would remember every day for the rest of her life. On her deathbed, in a hospital and alone in a twist of white sheets and various cords, she would be visited by the memory: the strange light, the wind in the trees, the smell of balsam after rain. The vision would take her back to the moment her young son became something more than a little boy.

As I said, this was not so long ago. The woman, Anne, is dead now, having lived through a life more trying than some, less than others. Nevertheless, she did live, and to a nearly ripe older age. That she died with a heart hollowed by the pain of a question never answered does not cast her so far back in history. These sorts of things happen around us every day. Most questions are never answered. Instead they are washed back and forth in the swash of time, rolled over the rocks of existence until rubbed and muted by the next moment and the next until forgetfulness diminishes the mystery to a ghost of its former self, like a wink of dull glass on a cobble beach. And yet, on certain days, when the light is right, when the wind is in the trees, on the heels of the rain, we can spy the glass and hear the echo of the ghost.

Louis Morrison Garoux was the son of Anne Morrison and Alan Garoux. Anne's father grew up in the north country, just inland from the Lake, near the fork of a clear river running over granite rock. The Garoux were from a tiny town over the border, below Thunder Bay. Both Anne and Alan had grown up in suburbs of cities far away from the Lake and any memory of the Big Water was strictly in the blood. But perhaps it was blood that called Anne and Alan to take the boy they so affectionately called Louie up the shore when he was still in diapers.

Louis was named for his great-grandfather, a fisherman working the Lake north of Grand Portage. Alan met his great-grandfather only once, when he was too young to remember nicotine-stained fingers, unruly silver hair, watery blue eyes or a small white frame house with a blank face turned to the setting sun on Pine Bay. Great-grandfather Louis spoke Français, and a little Norwegian, and "un peu Indienne." Today, one road leads to Pine Bay and it is called Memory Road, Route de Memoire or simply La Route, but Anne and Alan never knew even this.

So they took little Louie up the Shore. They stopped to camp at Split Rock, as people from the Cities are inclined to do. Their campsite sat high above Little Two Harbors, overlooking Ellingson Island with a view to the lighthouse. The campsite made Anne nervous. The fall from the cliff was precipitous. She did not want to let Louis out of her sight for a moment, but she did.

While Alan built a campfire, Anne sat Louis on his bottom and ducked into the tent for a hat for the baby's nearly bald head. She could not find the hat at first, and it took some moments to locate it at the bottom of a diaper bag. When she emerged from the tent, Louis was no longer sitting on his bottom, or sitting anywhere.

"Alan!"

Her husband turned from the fire.

"Louie! Where is Louie!"

Alan swept his dark hair back from his forehead and stared at his wife, momentarily uncomprehending.

"Oh, my God!" Anne's head swiveled, Alan began to call the child's name, and she turned on herself and raced for the rail at the cliff.

Below her, the waves washed and rolled large cobbles as they always do, but there was no small body, limp as a rag, in that swash.

Alan found him halfway down the campsite trail. Louis was sitting on his bottom, his hands slapping the wet mud above a small creek trickling through a culvert under the path. His father swept him up into his arms without noticing the fresh track in the mud beside the child's own prints.

Baby Louie grew faster after that first trip. His hair came in and his hands and feet began to lose their baby roundness. He crawled on his hands and knees and then he crawled on his hands and feet, bottom high in the air. Mother Anne called friends and finally visited the pediatrician. The doctor assured her that this was not unusual; many children crawled this way before walking and they should encourage the boy to stand, perhaps by offering his favorite foods. And so Anne stood in the small city kitchen, extending her arm, pinching a bit of bacon between her fingertips. Anne called to Louis and her son smiled and ambled over in his loping gait and then pushed himself up to a trembling stand like her childhood retriever, Custer. He opened his mouth, and without thinking, Anne placed the bacon between his new teeth. Later, awake in bed beside her sleeping husband, Anne would remember the moment and vow to ask for her son's hand instead.

Louis did eventually walk on two feet, like other children. Louis grew and played, mimicking his parents as best he could. A few years hence, another summer finally arrived after a particularly trying winter and the Garoux family decided to head up the Shore.

Seeking familiarity and forgetting the distress of their previous visit, they camped at Split Rock once more. Louis was out of diapers and running. The family camped at the foot of Little Two Harbors. It was not a conscious decision, avoiding the precipitous cliff, it simply happened. This latest campsite was crossed by a game trail and the park ranger warned them to keep the campsite clean and to place their food in the steel locker provided in order to discourage bears. Although they spoke about the nearness and coldness of the water, Anne and Alan had little need to worry about their son's safety. The boy was sure-footed and physically agile, and somehow, against their city natures, they trusted him, especially when they were away from their acquaintances at home.

At home, Louis was enrolled in a progressive preschool. Many well-educated parents of like minds sent their children to this school where much of the day was spent outside, in "nature," as they called it. These city people loved the idea of nature, so many acres so close to the city, but it was not in their natures to accept the risk inherent in a world not controlled by them. These parents did not abide danger and preferred a brand of wildness to true wilderness. Among these peers, the Garoux followed suit and worried openly about such things as ticks, mosquitos, probiotics and gluten. On their own, away from their peers, the parents knew that their son was capable and suspected his mind was quick. And yet, Louis gave them pause.

The boy's behavior showed intention and thought. They watched him build and rebuild complicated towers with blocks. They watched from the bay window of their house, without holding their breath, as Louis taught himself to climb the ash in the front yard. Louis had a terrific memory and his sense of direction was uncanny. When Anne was lost downtown, unable to find her way to the interstate, Louis simply said, "Turn, Mama," pointing correctly east. But the child did not talk much at all. He seemed to speak enough for his own purposes, but they worried and anticipated what his teachers would say. And the child balked. He balked at vegetables. He balked at pajamas and covers on his bed. He balked at forks and knives. Friends laughed and assured them that this was normal, even appropriate. But when the child balked, he did not so much squirm and complain as he howled in protest. The child howled so at the prospect of a scissor, for instance, that his black hair was much longer than his peers. He despised its being brushed as well, and so it was more unruly, too. The Garoux were often on guard in public with their son, and they were certainly reluctant to take Louis on an airplane. When they least expected it, when the boy encountered a situation that set him on edge, their son closed his dark eyes, tilted back his head, opened his mouth and simply howled.

The first night at the campsite was quiet and uneventful. The next day, the family woke, ate breakfast and headed for the trail. They planned to walk to the lighthouse and be back in time for lunch. It was early and windless. A light rain had fallen just before dawn and now the birds were active. Mist hung over the ground and the Lake, but the June sun seemed to be growing stronger, burning it away, and wood anemone bloomed on the greening forest floor. Anne and Alan walked and talked to their son, who trotted alongside. They pointed to the flowers and noted the birds. The child tossed his hair and kicked at the dirt and stones lining the path, then he swiped at his nose with the back of his hand and ran ahead.

"Not too far, Lou," called Anne.

Mother and father continued on, noting the whiteness of the bark on the trees, the diffuse light and the close quality of their voices in the strange weather. It was as if they were walking in a cloud. They were about to round a corner, expecting to see their son not far ahead, when Alan paused to re-tie his shoelace. Anne rounded the corner alone and what she saw stopped her in the wolf's tracks.

Louis lay on his side in the path and an animal stood above him, its paws straddling the boy's shoulders. A sudden light breeze pushed the mist back into the trees. The animal was a wolf and the boy was licking the corner of the wolf's muzzle with his own tongue.

Anne did not move or breath. She heard her son emit a sound like a whimper. His legs moved a bit, his feet pawing at the trail. The wind moved through her own hair. The boy braced his body with his forearms, tilting his head to reach the wolf. The wolf regarded Anne with intelligent water-blue eyes. It was clear that Louis was not afraid, but Anne was and she screamed.

By the time Alan arrived at her side, the wolf was gone and they stood watching their son roll in the dirt on his back, a smile on his face.

Anne could not speak about the wolf in her son's presence. She did not know why, but she could not. When Alan urged her to explain her scream, Anne could only shake her head and whisper, "I'll tell you later." The boy stood and shook himself off without looking at them and then trotted up the trail. Anne would keep him in sight for the rest of the weekend.

Later, after the boy had curled up in their tent, Anne stared into the dying fire and told her husband what she had seen. Alan could not believe her words. He believed his wife had seen something—their son playing with someone's dog, perhaps—but he could not believe his son had licked the mouth of a wolf. But the animal's gums were black. The teeth were white. In an even voice, his wife described the power and purpose in the body, the agouti fur, the eyes like water gazing at her with calm knowledge. Not a dog. A wolf. Simply a wolf. Anne did not sleep, but laid awake with one thought: *wolf.*

The trouble began during summer camp. Louis continued on at the progressive preschool after they returned from their trip Up North. The children played outside nearly all day and some of that time was spent in a sprinkler to enjoy the water and cool off. The children changed in and out of swimsuits for this play. Once out of his swimsuit, Louis refused to put clothes back on. A sheepish teacher called to report that Louis was "having a hard time today," and Anne could hear her son's defiant howl in the background. The sound traveled over the phone straight to her nervous system, electrifying her spine.

When she picked up her son that afternoon, the same teacher reported, more sheepishly, that, "Louie also peed in the sandbox." The teacher grimaced and added, "On another child."

Anne turned red, suddenly feeling the eyes and ears of the other parents in the chaos of the room. Anne insisted on knowing the name of the child, but the nanny had already left with him and so she forced herself to call the mother at home that evening. Anne did not know this mother and was grateful, but not reassured, when the woman laughed and said, "Please don't worry about it. These things happen."

But this mother was not so happy when her son was bitten by Louis. She said, "I'm sorry, Anne. Your son must be going through something, but, you know, he's scaring my kid."

Anne said she would call the pediatrician and did.

"Biting is pretty typical," said the doctor. Louis sat on the exam table, shirt off, kicking his legs. "We commonly see it in younger kids." Anne looked at the list of questions on the small yellow piece of paper in her hand. The doctor cleared his throat. "How old is Louis now?"

Anne was disappointed that she had to tell the doctor and when she said, "Four," the doctor winced.

"Yeah. That's a little old for typical biting. What does the teacher say?"

The teacher had said, "That's a little bit old for the typical biting behavior." Anne told the doctor, looked at him and said, "He also peed on another child. And he doesn't like to wear clothes." She swallowed. "He howls."

Anne knew that her son howled in displeasure, but his teachers had not yet found a way to tell her about a recent discovery. Louis often stopped and froze in the classroom, as if listening, and then he would howl. The women spoke of this anomaly in hushed tones at the end of the day, when they were alone in the classroom. And then one day, while Louis was howling, one teacher opened a window and heard the familiar sound of an ambulance. She looked at Louis and then she turned to her colleague, who was ready to meet her eye: Louis was howling with the siren. "Like a dog," said one woman to the other.

The doctor turned, squatted and looked Louis in the eye, "How come you peed on that kid?"

Louis tossed his head and sniffed. "Keeps taking my toys."

The doctor laughed and stood up, patting Louis on the shoulder. "That sounds pretty typical."

Anne didn't laugh. "But do we need to take him somewhere? Talk to somebody?"

"I'd hold off on that for a while. See if this resolves itself." The doctor looked at her. "Mom, you and Dad and the teachers can help Louie use his words. Just remind him." The pediatrician looked at his watch, not at Anne's son. "Non-verbal communication is still pretty typical for kids at this age."

Louis was fairly happy at the progressive preschool, especially when he was outside. But he tended to try to dominate the other children. On hikes, Louis insisted on running ahead first and refused to wait for his teachers. The boy rarely slowed down, but when he did, it was for scat. Louis took a great interest in animal scat, crouching and poking it with a stick, sometimes even bending low to give it a sniff. Back inside, Louis often couldn't sit still during story time and turned in circles or scratched at the rug before settling down. Sometimes he closed his eyes and curled up while the teacher read a book. He appeared to be sleeping, but often he could recall the details of the story with great accuracy. Every so often, Louis got into fights with other children, usually boys who challenged his right to toys. When Louis decided that one little girl should be his constant companion, he walked around holding her wrist and snarled at children who also wanted to play with her. Eventually the girl's mother complained and Louis was instructed not to touch her. For several weeks after this intervention, Louis kept to himself and, when the children were inside, he curled up in a corner of the classroom and closed his eyes.

Elementary school was harder for Louis and for Anne and, finally, for Alan. Louis was sent to the principal's office for peeing on the playground. His hair grew even longer, and other children teased him, asked him if he was "a girl." Louis retorted with his body, bloodying noses and scratching skin. After the third fight, Alan wept in the principal's office and a referral was made to a psychologist. Louis began to visit her on Thursday afternoons. He drew while the psychologist talked. He drew rabbits and squirrels and chipmunks and skunks. He drew with such intensity and skill that the psychologist recommended that Anne and Alan find an art class for their son. So Louis went to art class on Tuesdays and continued to visit his psychologist on Thursdays.

Louis did not do well on standardized tests and he did not like to talk in school, but his writing was very detailed and his teachers believed his comprehension was good. The psychologist administered a battery of tests and found that Louis was what she called "gifted" and the school agreed. Louis was enrolled in the programs for such children and somehow stayed out of the principal's office for months at a time.

Anne worried about her son's lack of friends and about his eating habits. The boy sometimes gorged, eating two or three school lunches a day. The school lunch bill was never consistent. And then sometimes Louis did not eat for what seemed like days. The boy refused to eat most vegetables and fruits, with the exception of berries, which he ate with enthusiasm, staining his teeth, lips and hands blue or purple. And Louis seemed to live for protein, the fattier the better. He relished the skin of roasted chicken, and preferred his meat soft, pliant and juicy. Louis would sneak and peck at roasting meat before it was fully cooked, then he would crack bones in his teeth at the dinner table. Anne worried about parasites and choking.

During these years, the Garoux family returned to the Shore every summer in June. First they stayed for a week, and then the next year, for two weeks. Eventually they rented a cabin not far from Split Rock for an entire month, with Alan coming and going from his job on the weekends. The cabin was spacious and homey, but Louis preferred to sleep in the tent he asked his father to help him pitch in the yard. On these trips, Louis was clearly happy. He disappeared for many hours at a time and returned very dirty, but he always returned. He sat and ate with his parents and talked more to them than he did at any other time of year. He told them about the loons fishing at the mouth of the river, about the frogs in the shallows, the toads under the rocks, the snakes by the waterfall, the taste of wild strawberries and the smell of the balsam on the ridge. And so they returned to the Shore, year after year.

On these trips, Anne tried not to think about what else Louis might do when he was alone in the woods. Once, Anne came across her son's sketchbook. She hesitated and then she began to thumb through it. There were drawings of trees, flowers, grasses. A raven. Then she found the wolves. There seemed to be two distinct animals. One with darker fur, one with lighter, mottled coloring. There were careful studies of ears, eyes, muzzles, paws and tails. The more complete portraits conveyed personality. One animal looked into the distance, but seemed to be aware of the artist's gaze. The darker wolf looked right into the viewer's eyes with a look of calm understanding. On subsequent pages, she discovered lively depictions of pups, rolling in grass and wildflowers. Anne put the book away and said nothing.

One evening, midweek, when Alan was in the Cities, Anne was cooking a late dinner when she froze. She had heard something. She was about to cross the room, move to the open window, when she heard it again. Down near the Lake. A loon? No. It was a call, but long, low, then high. Barking. The hair on her arms rose. More barking, closer to the cabin, it seemed. She moved to the open window and saw something in the fading light. Louis. He was coming up the path, looking over his shoulder. Were the bushes moving over there, off to the left? She saw that the boy was soaking wet, carrying his shirt and shoes in one hand. Anne backed away from the window and Louis came through the door. Water dripped from his hair, beaded on his fine collarbones and fell to the pine floor.

"You're soaking wet."

The boy grinned with his healthy white teeth. "I went for a swim."

"Louie! Aren't you freezing?"

Her son shook his head, spraying his mother with water. She snapped the dish towel at him. "Louis!"

He did it again and laughed. "I'm not cold at all!"

When he entered middle school, Louis discovered a love for cross-country running. He ran faster than any other boy and soon he was training with the high school team. Louis ran and spent a lot of time in the clubhouse he had built for himself in the backyard. One night he begged to sleep in his clubhouse, and after that it became a routine: on the weekends Louis slept in his clubhouse. Alan said, "Oh, Anne, he's a *boy*."

One day, in spring, near the end of Louis's eighth grade year, Anne received a call at work. It was the principal, asking if she could please come in and pick up her son.

When Anne walked into the office, she found Louis slouching in a chair with his eyes closed. "Hi, Mom," he said, without opening his eyes.

Across from Louis sat a girl, with her eyes open. She smiled at Anne. Her smile was knowing and sly. The girl swung a wall of dyed black hair over her shoulder. She wore too much makeup.

"Please come in, Mrs. Garoux," said the principal. To Louis she said, "Wait here. Mrs. Fairfax will keep an eye on you." And there sat the office secretary with her arms crossed, looking over her reading glasses. The girl with the wall of hair laughed. "Delaney, that's enough," said the principal.

It happened over lunch. Gottsacker, the track coach, hoping to catch the girl, Delaney, smoking, had walked to the edge of the woods. Delaney was indeed smoking, not far off the cross-country trail. When the coach approached her and began to reprimand her, the girl's eyes went wide and she laughed, interrupting him, "Check it out!" She motioned over the teacher's shoulder. Behind him, Louis was running down the trail, without a stitch of clothing on.

It was Alan who found the school. Northbound was up off the road to Finland, in the hills above the Lake. The program was called "Intercept." The promotional pictures showed grinning boys with long hair standing in a river, water up to their shins, arms slung around one another's necks. Louis was a year too young, but Alan talked the director into enrolling him. Louis's first expedition with Northbound was fifty days. Anne booked the cabin on the lake for two months and visited Louis at the school twice a week. Alan drove up and saw his son and wife on the weekends.

That first summer, the boy grew taller and stronger. His skin turned brown. His teeth looked whiter. One weekend, about a month and a half in, Louis introduced his parents to a girl. Her name was Susi. She was taller than Louis, and quite beautiful. She had delicately slanted eyes, prominent cheekbones, a fine blade of a nose, long blonde hair and pale blue eyes. She wore torn jeans and a large flannel shirt. She laughed easily and offered her hand to Anne and Alan in turn. When Susi looked at Louis, he blushed and her knuckles brushed the hem of his sleeve. Louis seemed happier than he had ever been. At the end of the summer, he asked his parents if he could enroll in the school that fall.

Louis never went to college. During his years at Northbound, the boy came to spend most of his time in the school's dog yard. He learned to run sled dogs and the director, a veteran musher, took Louis under his wing. When Louis was seventeen, and Susi eighteen, they crewed the director's Beargrease run. After the race, the musher presented Louis and Susi with a pup each. And so began Louis's life in the bush with Susi.

At first, they did not live together in the yurt, and their dogs stayed in the yard, training with the Northbound animals. Louis bunked in the yurt after graduation, while he worked as a musher and guide for the school. Susi lived in Grand Marais with her parents, working behind the family fish counter and driving down to visit Louis in the woods. In two more years, Louis bought the yurt from his mentor and Susi moved in. They took their two dogs and started their own dog yard.

When Anne and Alan went to visit their son in the woods above the lake, Anne felt like a stranger, like a tourist in their wilderness. Alan said little. The yurt was at the end of a long, old logging road. The road was so difficult that Anne and Alan had to park their sedan on the shoulder of Highway Six and wait for Louis to fetch them in his beat up, rusting truck. The yurt sat on a platform in the balsams overlooking a pond. No running water, only a stove and a small generator. They had an outhouse and a sauna. Wood was stacked in long rambling piles. Dog shit everywhere. Dog houses. Fifty-gallon drums of kibble. And everywhere there were dogs on chains, tethered to old axles, barking, howling, fighting, playing and sleeping. When Anne and Alan walked among the dogs, the huskies and malamutes, some barked, some growled, and others bared their teeth. But when their son walked among his pack, the animals rolled on their sides, displayed their stomachs and licked his hands eagerly.

In the ensuing years, Anne and Alan often traveled the old road to visit Louis and Susi at their dog camp, but they never stayed overnight. Eventually, Louis's parents bought the old cabin they had rented summer after summer. When they visited their son and Susi, they admired the new puppies and the ingenious homemade freezer dug into the ground and packed with pond ice where the couple froze garbage fish from Susi's family operation. They cross-country skied up there in the winter and enjoyed exhilarating sled rides with the fastest dogs, but they never felt like they belonged there at the end of the rough road. Susi and Louis lived with the woods, not in it. The pair seldom seemed cold and spent most of their time outside, only sleeping in the yurt. They wore their hair long and longer. Louis grew a beard. They smelled more like animals than people. They rarely wore gloves or mittens and their hands were strong and creased, the fingernails lined with dirt. Their bodies were lean and sinewy. They moved purposefully about the dog yard in scuffed boots, cuffing dogs on the ear or nuzzling them with open mouths. And with each other, the young couple displayed frankly physical affection. In his parents' presence, Louis kissed Susi full on the mouth, often taking her hair in his fist as he did. Susi would slip her hand beneath their son's shirt, rubbing his skin as she chatted with Anne and Alan about the beaver lodge on the pond. At the end of the day, Anne and Alan were relieved to return to their cabin by the Lake.

When Louis and Susi announced that they were having a child, Alan presumed they would move out of the yurt. Anne knew what Alan would ask before her husband opened his mouth. "Found a place yet?" Anne watched her husband's face as he held the phone to his ear. She gazed out the window at a torrent of rain, knowing that her son would stay in the woods with his pack of dogs.

When Susi's mother, Kirsti called, Anne was not surprised either. "She doesn't want to go to the hospital. I'm worried."

Anne told Kirsti she would try to talk to her son.

Kirsti sighed and was silent for a moment and then she said, "Anne?" She paused. It was late, dark. The storm was over and the moon was rising. "Do you ever wonder about them? About Lou, about Susi?"

Anne said, "How do you mean?" but she knew full well what Kirsti meant. She let the silence sit there, shouting through the darkness between them.

"Bud and I . . . Do you and Alan? I don't know. I'm just worried, that's all. Kids don't always do what you expect."

"No," said Anne, trying out a laugh. "They sure don't."

When she hung up, she weighed the phone in her hand. It seemed heavier, and foreign. An object she didn't understand. How could such a device transmit the thing in her heart through miles of darkness? Each of them were so lonely in their silence. But it was not a thing to talk about, let alone to understand.

What Louis told her on the phone should have surprised her also, but it didn't. "She's done it before. That's why she was at Northbound. She gave the baby up."

Anne held her breath. "Her mother is worried, Louis."

"She shouldn't be. Susi knows what she's doing. And I can help."

"You live at the end of a very long road, Lou."
"We'll be fine, Mom."

Faolan was not even born in the yurt, but out on the trail, in the open. Louis had to leave his wife's sled in the bush and mush back with Susi and the infant bundled into his sled. The snow was so deep, Kirsti couldn't get in for two days, and then only on the back of a snowmobile driven by Susi's father, Bud. It was a week before Anne and Alan could make the trip. Louis met them on the shoulder with a team and a sled. The baby was small and red, and when Anne looked into her watery blue eyes for the first time, she cried and thought about Susi's blood in the snow. Her son's knife. The placenta. What had the dogs done?

The baby slept curled up with a new puppy in a sheep-skin between her parents. As the girl grew, she thought of the white dog, Tasha, as her sister. And why not? Tasha did not sleep outside, she slept in the yurt. Tasha was not picketed on an axle in the yard. She ate her fish from a plate inside, like the others. Faolan and Tasha swam in the pond and ran through the woods. When Anne and Alan visited, Tasha and their grand-daughter sat side by side, listening with heads cocked, each gaz-ing with clear blue eyes. When Alan tossed Faolan into the air, Tasha barked and cavorted at his side.

Faolan grew to closely resemble her mother, with fine fea-tures, a distinctive nose and those watery blue eyes, but her hair was dark like her father's. Susi nursed Faolan until she was nearly four years old and once, after dinner, when her grandpar-ents were sitting and visiting with her parents, they were sur-prised to see the tall child enter the yurt with her dog, skillfully and quickly unbutton her mother's shirt, find her breast and begin to nurse. The dog sat at the child's side, bored and panting with a lolling, wet, pink tongue. As she suckled, Faolan kept an eye on her grandfather while he searched for a way to continue the conversation. When she was done, the child wiped her mouth with the back of her hand, buttoned her mother's shirt and said, "Come on, Tashi." In silence, Anne and Alan watched the girl bang out the door of the yurt. Anne heard barking. The dog? More barking. Faolan. And then the girl and Tasha, the dogs in the yard, and the others in the woods, began to chorus. Their howls rose, carrying the sound of yearning up through the falling darkness.

GREAT GRAY

I.

Ice. The Big Lake. Frozen in mountains, ridgelines, abrupt saw-tooth eruptions. Giant broken plates of ice scatter like the aftermath of a colossal tantrum. Around another bend, looking down, pancakes of ice float, frilled with crenelated edges, like Amazonian lilypads. Then another vista opens on to a vast, flat, windswept expanse. One long fissure zigzags into the distance. Then broken mirrors of ice, but the scale is jarring. Ice, rising and leaning stories into the blue sky. Islands of ice, like new headlands. They cast blue-green and purple leeside shadows. Nina's eyes brim with tears. So much beauty. Sunglasses do little to cut the relentless, breath-taking glare. She drives down and west, new worlds of ice around each corner, just out there, beyond the windshield, through naked birches. All that frigid, clear air between the hurtling van and the lake. The air seems so thin, so precise. Maybe sharp enough to cut like a knife and draw blood. Despite her own history, despite her existence, the world continues to unfold, moment by moment, in relentless, indifferent beauty. Nina thanks a god, if there is one, for eyes to see Lake Superior on this morning in early March.

II.

He sits high in the pine, facing west. His chest heaves and his eyes dilate in the dazzle of sunlight on snow. The flight from

Palisade, away from the mobbing ravens, had cost too much. His body is on fire, the muscle consuming itself, devouring his very bones. He burns white hot from the inside out and in a flash of immolation, he sees his mate. So much larger than himself, magnificent in her dominion, she spreads her great gray wings wide in greeting. She is as vast as the slate Lake. She takes him to the breast of the setting sun and he is an owlet again, warm once more in the crush of mother feathers.

III.

Some part of Nina actually sees the bird fall. As she drives past Palisade Head, she clocks the Great Gray laying in the snow, it's wings spread wide. It is only after she pulls over, takes up her camera, straps on her snowshoes and treks over the saddle of deep ditch snow that she realizes she in fact saw the owl drop from the high branch.

Nina takes off her sunglasses and squints down at the magnificent bird. She removes a mitten and kneels. Her fingertips burn with cold. She hesitates to touch the animal. The wide yellow eyes stare through who she is: forty-three, a mother, alone. Already, the liquid of the eyes seems to be clouding, the jelly freezing. The Gray's talons, feathered to the tips, curl around nothing in a rictus of longing. Nina moves her bare hand, catches her breath and holds it, touches the feather at the tip of the wing.

The bird is dead. She is sure. And yet. Nina puts on her mitten. The owl is stiff. But she saw it fall. Must have died on the limb. Dead on the perch for some time. She waits for her hand to come back to life inside the cocoon of mitten. She suddenly removes both mittens, unzips her parka and takes up the camera around her neck. She knows the machine will quickly turn sluggish in the cold. She leans in close. One eye. The black pupil a portal to the brain, to the animal that was. The yellow iris actually contains green and crystal bars of gold. A skim of film is forming around the very edges of the black lid. The camera begins to freeze up. Nina's fingertips sear with cold and she longs to put them in her mouth, but knows this is a bad idea.

She zips the camera back into her coat and shoves on her mittens. As she turns away toward the road, the van and the expanse of hard china-blue sky, her eye catches the tip of the gray feather on white snow, the fine pattern of minute quills, so much like the vein in a leaf or the row of needles on a balsam. Nina sees history in the grain of crystalline snow, particles of ice, air married to water and frozen in time. Nina swears, for the fact of the frozen camera. So many things in this world are held in the eye only and will never be recalled so perfectly again.

Nina puts on her sunglasses and returns to the car. She throws her snowshoes in the back. Back in the driver's seat, she turns the car on. She shivers convulsively and waits for the heater to kick in. Across 61, the back of Palisade, stubborn hunk of lava, rises up into all that blue sky. The bird turned its back on the monolith, turned away from the mid-morning sun.

Nina opens the glove compartment, but does not find what she needs there. She reaches under the front seats, then turns and rummages through gear piled in and around the back seats. Finally, she gets out of the warming van, walks to the back and throws open the hatch. She pushes through snowshoes and poles, spare boots, the box of books, her backpack, thermos, water bottle, sleeping bag and pillow. Then her eye falls upon the long, clear, plastic box that contains Mark's plaid wool hunting shirt. She pulls the box out of the mess. Nina does not know why she still keeps the box with his shirt in the van. It has been a year since she sold the house, since she moved the boys into the apartment. She does not know where to put the box. She pictures the third floor apartment, crammed to overflowing with the boys' sports equipment, books, clothing, legos. She has stuffed every nook and cranny with a whole house worth of things. It is all too much for an apartment to hold. The place cannot contain the old life and it spills out of closets, trips her on the stairs and lies in wait under the beds.

Nina takes off her mittens and removes the stiff lid from the box. Mark was a tall man, with broad shoulders. The muscles of his back moved under the fabric of his t-shirt, so alive, coiling with strength. That last summer, when they were working on the house, sweat curled the light hair at the nape of his tanned neck. The smell of her husband is suddenly there in the clear, cold air, the molecules radiating from his favorite shirt. Wood smoke and Russian pipe tobacco. The wool is cold. Nina's nose begins to run, but she holds the rough material to her numb face. She smiles and her eyes fill with water. She walks back to the driver's side as a car streaks by. She opens the door and drapes the shirt on the back of her seat then closes the door, returns to the back hatch and straps on her snowshoes again. The pain in her fingertips is terrible. She puts her mittens on once again and climbs up across the saddle of deep snow.

Nina crouches and hesitates. Those eyes. She looks over her shoulder. No cars. She finds that the wings oblige the pressure of her hands and fold into the body as she desires. The dark to light striations of the feathers radiating out from the eyes, the careful mottling of the blacks and grays down the breast, the curve of the yellow beak, the fierce design so perfect in purpose — it is all too much beauty to leave behind. The bird is so light, it is a surprise. The owl looks so impressive, but the weight of the bird is a revelation exposing the trick to her mind. The bird feels like so much nothing. It is perfect. Her heart races as she cradles the body in her left arm and crosses the ditch as quickly as she can. She hears a truck and trips to the hatch of the van as the big semi gains the ridge. She lays the bird in the now-vacant plastic box, rips off her mittens with her teeth and snaps on the stiff lid.

A sarcophagus. That's what it looks like. In the rearview mirror, she can see the owl in the plastic bier, perched atop the debris of her life. She should have put it down low, under the sleeping bag or pillow. It is too easy to see.

The maw of the Silver Creek tunnel looms ahead and she turns her eyes to the task of the road. As the van enters the dark tube, Nina hears a strange sound, sees something. Not outside, but in her vehicle. Her eyes flutter to the mirror, the box slides. Does the dark shape in there move? A moving company semi approaches. Suddenly the van explodes with movement, a beating of wings, a splitting, screeching sound hits Nina's brain like a stab, travels down her spine in spikes of fear and her white hands on the wheel react. The van swerves. The yellow-green eye, the black iris, the portal — these are the last things Nina will ever see.

Van and semi collide. The impact hurls the van into the tunnel wall. The van spins and leaps out into the sun and Nina is thrown through the windshield, through the sharp air, into the clean snow. The owl follows through the jagged exit hole and hits the wind lifting off the Lake. It flies into the china-blue sky, higher and higher.

Nina woke in darkness, an ungodly pain filling her head and working out in waves through her extremities.

"Momma! Momma!"

Ellis. She reached out and could not find him in the dark. She was not awake. Not awake. "Mark, turn on the goddamned lights." This she said aloud, thinking it was a dream.

"Gramma!" Eddie was upset, in need, crying. "Gramma!"

"Boys, she doesn't know."

Her mother. Her boys. All of them. Almost. She was awake. Then, like a movie, Nina put her hands on her face and found the bandages covering her eyes. Wads of slightly damp stuff pressed into the sockets.

"Nina, honey, we are so glad you're here."

Her father too. Then her mother, smelling of lavender. Nina found her mother's face and it was wet, with tears running into her mouth. "It was bad, honey," she said. "Very bad."

Her boys found her hands and then their bodies were there in the bed, pressing hot and bony against her broken limbs.

"You'll walk." That's what the man said. Not the doctor. The OT. The doctor was a woman. She was the one who said, "No serviceable vision."

"I won't see." Nina said this to the OT. He smelled something like clove, and something sharp like lime.

"But you'll walk," he retorted. Then he pulled her up roughly, making her sit up without pillows. She felt like a rag doll. He was manhandling her. She didn't want to sit up. And he forced her. She hated him.

The doctor said Nina's eyes would only sense light and darkness. That was all. She would never really see anything again, only "discern the suggestion of darker shapes." It was like being in a dream, or at the bottom of the sea with too much water between her and the surface. She would never swim up to the surface. Like a nightmare. She imagined the primordial eyes of early reptiles. She once read about the vestigial third eye of iguanas. They only sensed light and dark, alerting the reptilian brain to the ariel shadow of the predator, setting flame to the flight response. Nina sometimes knew when people or things were near, but she could not navigate anymore. Her compass was gone. She had no bearings at all without her hands and limbs, which were compromised to a ridiculous point. Her hands were clumsy, several fingers on each bound together in splints like rudimentary claws. And her legs were heavy, unwilling logs. Her legs were dumb wood, sluggish to the point of unresponsiveness, and yet, amazingly, they hurt, god damn it. She gave up on caring about her legs and wished they'd fall off or go completely numb. It was all a pain. Too much bother. Nina suddenly laughed, an ugly barking sound like a seal.

"What are you laughing at?"

The OT. He was mad. She could hear the cold irritation in his voice.

He held her shoulders and gave her a small shake. "What's so funny?"

She laughed again. "Not a fucking thing is funny." She barked. "First my husband dies of an aneurysm. Now I'm fucking blind, and a cripple."

"Nina! The boys are here!"

Why hadn't she at least smelled them? She wanted to vomit.

"Today you are going to do some leg lifts." Again with the clove and citrus.

"You smell like an aftershave commercial."

"Thank you. Stop slouching, okay?" His hands were vices. She imagined them as big as baseball gloves.

"Do the ladies like that shit?"

"My aftershave? Oh, sure. And they like it that I shower. You know what a shower is, right? It's this great invention: water, soap, shampoo. Gets you nice and clean. Gets the stink off of you."

"You're an—"

"A real gentleman, right?" He took her right ankle in his hands and lifted her leg straight up.

"Jesus Christ!" She could smell his hair as he bent her knee. And then she could see Mark's hair, or imagine it, like a photograph.

"No pain, no gain."

"That really, really hurts." She would not cry now.

"The truth hurts. Take a shower, Nina."

After he left, she ran her claws through her hair. It was greasy and matted. Her mother had fought with her about the shower. She had brought up the boys, said she didn't want them to see her like that. They had even had a small tussle when her mother had tried, with the help of a nurse, to give her a sponge bath. The three of them ended up damp and enraged and the nurse had sicced a psychiatric resident on her. The resident sounded like she was about fifteen. Nina could hear her flipping through interview questions. It was all so canned, so pro forma. Nina told her to "get the fuck out of my room." The girl sputtered and the papers ruffled, some maybe fell to the floor. It sounded like the kid had to scoop them up before she exited. Nina could picture a small pointed face, hair the color of nothing, transparent skin and a cheap watch on the girl's thin wrist. She felt bad about this for a moment, but then she realized she had so much more to feel bad about and Nina laughed like the hag she had become.

The bastard was making her sit up again, jerking her left leg up and down. She had debated the merits of her plan and she almost didn't bring it up, but then he said, "You actually don't smell like an old lady today, Nina. Congratulations."

She ignored him. "Do you know where the Silver Creek tunnel is? On Highway 61?"

"Why? You planning a trip?"

"Do you want to make some money?"

"Thanks, but I already have a job." He dropped her leg suddenly.

"Ow!"

"You can anticipate and control movement, Nina. It's your body." He took her right ankle, lifted and then applied pressure to her heel, moving her hip in its socket. He pushed what must have been his thumb into the arch of her foot.

"Jesus!"

"No, I told you, my name is, Jack." He kneaded her calf, hard.

"I'll pay you two hundred bucks, plus gas, to drive up to the Silver Creek tunnel and look for my camera. It'll only take a half-day. If you find it, I'll give you another hundred."

"You should be more careful with your things, Nina."

"Come on, John, or whoever you are. I need that camera."

"Sorry. I'm busy. And my name is Jack."

Nina pulled her leg out of his grasp. It hurt like hell, but she was done.

"Ooo. Very good. Nice control!"

"Go away, John."

He did. He left without another word and left her in the chair. She had to go to the bathroom. The call button was too far away. When she tried to get out of the chair, she fell down. This frightened her so much that she pissed herself. She crawled to the bathroom on her hands and knees, trailing urine and snot.

"Where's John?"

"You mean Jack?" This OT was a woman. She sounded small. Her hands were wiry and she smelled like Ivory. "I believe Jack is out sick."

Nina laughed. "Good."

The woman made a *tsk, tsk, tsk* sound. "Oh, Jack's the best there is. He's a real nice guy." The little bird woman clamped on to her leg and moved it this way and that with apparently very little effort. "Now, you've got to resist me. I'm going to bend that knee of yours and you're going to resist, all right?" She bent, Nina tried to resist, but found she could not. The tiny woman was as strong as an ox. "All right, again!" Again and again, Nina tried and failed to resist the little drill sergeant. "Jack said you were a tough nut to crack, but you're just about as tough as a stick of butter." She slapped Nina lightly on the thigh. "Watch out now, can't let yourself get all flabby. That Jack's a real looker, you know. Handsome Jack!"

She wanted to tell her she couldn't "watch out" and was unable to see that any man was a "real looker," but she held her tongue. Her boys were due any minute.

The birdy OT came again the next day, reporting that Jack was "still sick." Nina made an attempt to do what the woman asked of her for what she guessed was at least ten minutes. Then she just stopped, but the woman, Elise, persisted. "Nina, my name is Elise Rose McCarthy and I've been an occupational therapist for more than twenty years. I usually work with kids who have degenerative diseases, that's my specialty. I try to help them remain mobile while their bodies deteriorate. So I work with children who are fighting to keep moving while their bodies are rotting out from under them. And here I am today, helping out my good friend Jack, forcing you to move a body that you are willfully letting deteriorate. You do not have a degenerative disease, just a degenerative point of view."

Nina listened to the silence settle around them. She paid attention to the light she could sense beyond her bandaged eyes. "Well. Thank you very much, Elise."

The next morning, Nina's mother came into the room, smelling like something alive. "I've got flowers. Lily of the valley, in a pot. Smells like spring." She placed the pot in Nina's lap. "Got your dad to the airport okay." The delicate perfume of the flowers and their dirt wreathed her head. Fragile lily of the valley would never survive out in Arizona, in her dad's backyard. Something else was dropped at the foot of the bed.

"What's that?"

Her mother took a deep breath and sat down on the edge of the bed. "Don't you want to know how the swim meet went last night?" The boys had returned to school and their regular activities. Homework, tests, swim meets. Life went on. Her mother was working so hard to make it all normal for the boys. The enormity of this effort, this selflessness, this love was so much, so embarrassing, so heavy, Nina could only ignore it and hate herself a little bit more.

"What's on the bed?"

She felt her mother stand and then remove the pot of flowers. "Hold out your hands." It was a command, something a mother said to a too-expectant child. Nina heard a zipping sound, a crinkle like plastic and she knew what it was before it fell into her hands. Wood smoke. Russian tobacco.

"It was full of glass," said her mother. "He picked all the shards out, folded it so nice and put it in this bag. Your blood's all over it."

And there it was, like iron in her nose, crusting under her prying fingernails.

"He knows you went through the windshield and the shirt had so much glass in it. And that big rip." She took Nina's right hand and helped her find the tear. "He thinks it probably saved you from severing an artery in your neck."

"Who thinks that?"

"Nina, I have your camera. I've had it. It was still in the van. I didn't want you think about your pictures, about photography." Her mother began to cry.

Nina didn't say anything when Jack came in. She waited, but he said nothing, just took her elbows then slung her arm over his shoulder. His other arm went around her waist and he straightened up. They stood hip to hip for a moment. So he was her height. Her legs shook with effort. She struggled to lock her knees. Her stomach muscles strained. She clenched her teeth and held onto the round muscle of his shoulder for what seemed like dear life.

"Now you are going to learn to walk to the bathroom. So you don't piss yourself again."

"I didn't know my camera wasn't there."

"I know."

"You went."

"I did."

"It was his shirt."

"Your mother told me."

"He was my husband." And to her embarrassment, Nina began to cry. She trembled in her pajamas and wept. "I'm going to fall."

"You won't."

Jack came at ten thirty each morning. If Nina sat in the chair by the window, she could put one hand on the cold pane while she practiced leg lifts. First, the sun fell on her face and then when it reached her neck, it was time for Jack to come. He knocked once and entered without waiting. His shoes squeaked on the floor. She could heard the fabric of his scrubs as he crossed the room and she imagined they were blue. He had a pen that he clicked before writing on her chart. Perhaps the ink was black. He had hair on his forearms and once her fingertips brushed the cold metal of his wristwatch, on his right wrist. He was left-handed.

On Wednesday, Jack came to Nina's room at one thirty.

"We're going on a field trip."

"Without a wheelchair?"

"Without a wheelchair."

That first afternoon, Jack walked her, very slowly, down the hall. They took the elevator to get to the therapy room on the floor below. Once in the elevator, the sudden lurch of the machine knocked Nina off balance and she felt like she was tipping off a precipice. It scared her so badly, she panicked and pawed the air like an animal. Jack caught her by the elbow and pressed his thumb into her bone so hard, she inhaled sharply in surprise.

"You need to breathe, Nina. Just breathe." She heard the doors slide open, felt a shift of air. "You got it. Go ahead."

Nina did not move.

"Just walk forward, and keep breathing."

The therapy room smelled like sweat and antiseptic. *In other words*, thought Nina, *it smells like fear*. Nina held on to the carpeted wall while Jack greeted another person, maybe a therapist too. "Sal," he called her. The woman smelled like a bath shop. It was the way she walked, the swish of her scrubs and her slight wheeze before she said, "Hi there," that told Nina that Sal was a big person. Jack reached across Nina to take something from Sal. The item clicked and stuttered on the floor between them.

"Hold out your right hand, " said Jack.

"Me or her?" said Nina.

"Very funny." Jack placed something with a handle in her hand. It took both hands and a few long moments and then it hit her. It was like a tent pole, but it was not for camping. "Ah. I see." *Said the blind woman,* she thought.

"You have to learn how to use one of these."

"Crap."

"It'll help."

"Do I get a tin cup too? How about some sunglasses?"

This made big Sal chuckle.

"Thanks, Sally. I'm trying not to reinforce that behavior."

Nina gripped the cane in her right hand and cast her left hand out, trying to find the carpeted wall again. "If I fall down in here, I'm going to get rug burn."

On Thursday, they took the stairs instead of the elevator. Jack made Nina carry the cane.

"What color is it again?"

"I'm not answering that question any more."

The chilly stairwell echoed, throwing sound around her head. Nina thought she was starting to feel sound with her whole body. Fish did that. "What if I don't want to do this today?"

"I'll leave you in here by yourself."

"No, really. What if I'm really just not ready?"

"What happens if there is a fire in your house some day? What happens if one of your boys is hurt and you're the only one at home? If you're not going to suck it up for yourself, do it because you are going to be a mother again someday."

"Like I'm not right now?"

"Right."

She thought about calling him a bastard, and then she did it. "You're a real bastard."

"Nope. My mom and dad were and are still married. Put the cane out in front of you. You're not Moses."

"Wait until I part the Red Sea."

"Funny. Now sweep it out in front of you and hold the railing with your other hand."

"It's cold in here."

"I'm right behind you. Go slow."

Nina felt the empty air behind her, the dangerous space over the railing. "Could you like hold on to my bathrobe or something?"

"Nah, this is your thing."

Suddenly Nina was enraged again. The feeling flooded hotly through her body, out to her fingertips. She whacked the first stair with the cane. "I'm sick of this shit."

"Me too."

On Friday, Jack came at ten thirty, as usual, but instead of exercising in the room, he told Nina to stand up. "Field trip," he said. "And then, if you're a good girl, hydro therapy."

"Hydro therapy?"

"Hot tub. For those screwed-up knees of yours. Let's go."

Nina stood up.

"Ooo. Sweats. Classy."

"Shut up."

"Let's go, Zumba girl."

Nina followed Jack toward the door, and then he let the damn thing fall closed right on her cane.

"Christ!"

"Use it or lose it," he called from the hallway.

Jack stayed a few steps in front, always just out of reach. He let her crash into things and collide with people. Nina could not keep track of where they were going. She pictured a maze, with a rat. She began to sweat. The pace Jack set, she knew, was nothing more than a snail might keep, but her heart raced as if she were running. She heard more people, different sounds, felt a rush of cold air.

"Where are we?"

"You tell me."

"Entrance?"

"Maybe. Go ask."

"Ask what?"

"Go over to the information desk and ask where you are."

"No way."

"Okay." And then Jack's voice was suddenly farther off. "See ya."

Nina took a step in the direction of his voice and bumped into something. A potted plant. Someone brushed by her. "Excuse me." Nina thought she might not be able to stop herself from crying. And anybody out there, around her, would see her contorted face, see her and feel pity. The poor blind woman. She was blind. With a cane! She touched the bandages. When they came off, her eyes would probably roam around in her head in that way. She would have that sunken, black circle look. She never wanted the bandages to come off, ever. "Shit."

Nina listened for a minute, then she turned her back on the plant. She could feel outside air and hear outside noises periodically. Cars and a general roar of the world out there, like a great, constant vacuum cleaner. People moved around her and she could smell the cold on them. She nosed the cane out in front and walked a few steps that way. She heard a phone ring out in front and then a woman said the name of the hospital. "How can I direct your call?"

Nina walked toward the woman with the phone. To Nina's right, a child laughed, a girl, and then footsteps, running. She must have caught a toe on Nina's cane because the cane jerked and the kid sounded like she stumbled and fell. The child made a little grunting noise. Nina froze.

"Amelia! Careful! You almost knocked this lady over."
Then the woman's voice came directly at Nina, in her face,
"Sorry!"

Nina unfroze. "No problem."

They moved off and Nina heard the woman say, "That
lady can't see, Amelia. She can't see people coming. You've got
to watch where you're going."

Nina had said, "Watch where you're going," so many
times to her own children. Never once did she think that some
people couldn't, even if they wanted to. People were so careless
with words. "See you tomorrow." That was another one. She
said it to Mark, when she was in Duluth for that evening. She
did see him the next day, but he did not see her. What was the
last thing Mark saw?

Nina took a step and then another and then her cane
bumped into something solid and she reached out her left hand
for what must be the desk.

"I'm over here, hon."

Nina turned to her right, toward that voice.

"You're at the security guard's podium."

Then Nina smelled the guy.

"Ma'am." His voice came from just above her forehead.
He was tall and maybe black, by the sound of his, "Ma'am," and
she must have been nearly on top of him.

Nina felt herself blush. "Sorry."

"No trouble."

Then the lady at the desk: "Can I help you?"

"Where am I?"

"South entrance on Smith. Ground floor. Jack is waiting
for you in the cafeteria, Nina."

"Nice trick."

She thought she could hear Jack grinning.

"You look a little sweaty. How about some ice cream to celebrate?"

"Celebrate what?"

"You're graduating. McGrath is going to tell you that you're shipping out day after tomorrow."

Nina felt the last bit of air leak out of her.

"You don't look so happy."

Nina realized she was sitting on the edge of her chair, clutching the cane tightly with both hands. "I'm just really tired."

Jack cleared his throat. "Well," he snuffled as if rubbing his nose, "I was gonna make you get your own ice cream, but I think I'll do the honors. Chocolate or vanilla."

"Coffee."

"Gross. I hate coffee ice cream."

When Jack returned with the ice cream, they worked on their cones in silence. Nina licked the vanilla soft serve and listened to conversation around them. Chairs scraped the floor. Someone blew their nose, maybe a man. Cash register. A woman laughed.

Nina said, "What flavor did you get?"

"Coffee."

"You did not."

"Wanna lick?" And suddenly the ice cream was under her nose and she could smell it: coffee.

"You are a bastard."

"I was waiting for you to smell it."

Nina managed to bite the cone right out of Jack's hand.

When Nina left the hospital, she went to live with her mother and her boys. Jack was no longer her therapist. Her mother drove her to a clinic where she worked with a large pillowy woman named Violet. Violet smelled, oddly enough, like Obsession perfume. Her hands were gentle and she said all the right things. Nina worked on building strength, coordination, and using the cane. She was supposed to start the other kind of therapy at the end of the week.

During the day, while her mother was at work and the boys were at school, Nina tried to find her way around her childhood home. She called her father in Arizona and asked him if he remembered how many windows were in the living room, what color the basement floor was, where the tennis rackets and skis used to be stored. Her father and mother had been divorced for more than ten years, but he remembered as they talked. Together, they worked to fill in holes and gaps.

One day, her father said "I used to store the spare house key up on top of the lantern by the back door."

Later that day, Nina called him with the news that it was still there, she had found it. She felt triumphant. Her dad said, "Oh, I miss that old house. It was a good one." And then the silence laid down across the distance and the weight of history bore down. Her father said, "He was a good man, Nina." And her father listened while Nina cried and when she stopped, her father told her he would see her in a week and then he caught himself and he cried. Nina listened to him stop and take a deep breath. "You didn't do it on purpose, did you, honey?"

She laughed then. "No. I was looking at a bird, Dad. I got distracted." The last statement was a lie. Distraction was no way to describe what had happened that day. She had been paying attention, paying so much attention. "Just fate, I guess," she said.

One afternoon, she found a heavy book on the shelf in her mother's bedroom closet. The smell of it was familiar. Old paper and sticky plastic page covers. It was of course the family album. Pictures of her own babyhood, her married parents, her sister, Eliza, alive, but now dead. Her dog, Buster, long gone. Now she would never even see those imperfect pictures of Eliza, of Mark. Nina pulled the pictures out of their sleeves, pressed them to her face, smelled the images and no more, no more. The rage came out of nowhere again and nearly knocked her flat. She struggled to breathe and tried to pull the bandages from her head, to get her eyes free, to try, try, try, try to see anything at all.

She had to find a scissors. She dumped an entire drawer of unknown crap out on the kitchen floor. She crawled through the mess, flailing, trying to lay her hands on something sharp to sever the goddamned bandages. And then the doorbell rang.

Nina froze.

It continued to fill the air with crazy, insistent, stupid bonging. She didn't give a shit! Raging, insane with anger, she stumbled toward the door without her cane, banging her hip hard on an end table, tripping over a chair leg, blistering the air with expletives.

She swung the door open and leaned into the cold, anticipating the exchange of violent sounds to come.

"Hi, Nina."

Clove and lime. She inhaled.

"I'm sorry this is so out of the blue."

Nina stepped back, hanging hard on the door. "How did you get here?"

"Car."

"I mean, how did you find me?"

"I had your mother's number. I called her."

"Okay."

"She said it was okay."

"What's okay?"

"It's cold out here. I have something for you."

Nina stepped back again, far enough, she thought, to let Jack through. As he passed into her house, she smelled the down of his jacket and felt the cold falling from his body. "What color is your hair?"

"What makes you think I have hair?"

"What color is it?"

"Dark brown."

"Okay."

He moved farther into the house. "Looks like you took out a chair or two."

"You should see the kitchen."

"Can I help you with something?"

"I was looking for scissors."

"I asked your mom for the camera."

Nina stayed very still. Her heart beat in her throat. She wanted to hang on to something, but she didn't know what, so she put her hands on her hips.

"I made prints."

Jack made a noise, shifting something in front of him. The packet of photographs.

"You're a good photographer, Nina. He was really something. Really beautiful."

She saw Mark, or pieces of him, in her mind. His mouth, his wrist and the blond hairs there, his hand and wedding band, the veins in the back of his hands, his knuckles. "Tell me."

Jack came close to her, his breath nearly in her own mouth. She stood in her bare feet on the brick tile of the entryway. Jack put a photograph in her hand. "The black around the eye is like eyeliner. So dark. The gray feathers are very fine, like hair. The eye is yellow like the color of lake water in summer. There is green in it and flecks of gold. And I can see a tiny you, Nina, reflected in his eye. You are in the eye, with the camera just under your nose. You are looking into the owl's eye and I can see you looking."

Nina did not dare to touch him. "Help me find some scissors. Please help me find some scissors."

She heard him walk away from her, back into the kitchen, creeping through the mess. Then he returned and she held out the photograph.

"You hold on to that," he said. He touched her lightly and gently pulled at the bandage allowing enough clearance to slip the blade between her skin and the webbing. He was done in two strokes and then it was down to the wads of cotton over her eyes. "When was this supposed to come off?"

Her mother had helped her change the dressing every day in a darkened room. Her mother had rinsed her lids with a solution, pulled out each lower lid and squeezed a drop into each. Nina had worked hard to keep her eyes closed. She had not wanted to try to see, to look for light or shadow. "Tomorrow." It was true, the appointment to examine her eyes was set for the morning.

Jack waited.

"I won't see anything."

"I know."

She pulled the wadding away from her damp, sticky lids. "Are they open?"

"Yes."

Jack waited.

"If that's you, you're dark." She reached out and let her hand graze his jacket. He did not move. "And I guess it's lighter over here," she gestured. "But it's just shadows and light, like I saw before, when I closed my eyes, when I could see."

Jack is still.

"What do they look like?"

He is still for a moment longer. Nina shakes and seems to fight to lock her knees, to try to root herself through the cold floor. Her long hair falls down over her shoulders, tangling down her back, the curling amber tendrils shaking as her body shakes. Her bare feet are pink with blood, the veins snaking blue across the arch of each foot. Jack takes Nina by the elbows and lifts her weight from her trembling knees. They are exactly the same height. He can smell toothpaste on her breath. Her teeth are large and straight on the top, crowded and crooked on the bottom. Her lower lip is slightly chapped, as if she has been biting it. He wraps one arm around her waist, to hold her up while he tilts her chin with his thumb and forefinger. Her skin is pale, but her cheeks are flushed.

"Your irises are gray, like the feathers, with veins of white. The scars are like small rivers of ice. Your pupils are as big as they can be. Very black. And I can see a reflection of myself right there, in your eye."

ACKNOWLEDGMENTS

This book was written with the help of my family and friends and the people, flora and fauna of that particular part of the planet known as the North Shore of Minnesota and Chigamig, or Lake Superior.

My husband, Erik, and my children, Holly and J.J., helped me find the time, funds, and general support to write and range along the Shore. My family endured many hours in our car, accompanied by obsessional researching, reading and talking about all things Lake. Thanks to my good friend Bev for letting me show her "my North Shore," and for being one of the brightest rays of light in my life. Thanks to The Bird Club for simply understanding and giving me the courage to go for it. And thanks in particular to the muse K.N. for tolerating my writing voyeurism and "artistic" licenses. I could not have written this book without hearing the strong voices of some amazing women. The brave Angelique Mott, Ingeborg Holte, Beryl Singleton Bissell, Cathy Wurzer and Staci Lola Drouillard taught me much about writing and enduring. The "Northern Lights" of Howard Sivertson, Justine Kerfoot, Peter Oikarinen, and George Morrison continue to guide me. Alice Hoffman, who selected my very first story for publication many years ago, gave me permission, by virtue of her own writing, to embark on this book. I also owe much to storyteller Sean Fahrlander, Nisoasin, who helped me honor my Ojibwe friends and their culture with his precise and thoughtful edits, and generous encouragement. I would also like to thank Jeannette Henrikssen and her mother for reading the work with a Norwegian eye and ear. While these friends may have worked hard to help me get cultural details right, so as not to embarrass myself, any fumbles that remain are mine alone.

My gratitude will always extend to the late Richard Elman, who was my first and best mentor in the world of words and the human condition. Corinne, Curtis, and Anne at North Star gave me a great break, and I thank them for their candor, enthusiasm, and support. Thanks to my readers and booksellers Up North, and thanks to Betsy Bowen for generously opening the doors of her Grand Marais gallery for this book. I have a feeling that my parents, Jan and Dan, are gratified to see me in print again, and I thank them, and my brother, Aaron, for their steady belief that I should be a writer. I consider it a great stroke of luck that Noah Prinsen agreed to collaborate on this project. Noah's beautiful prints "speak" of matters of the heart and the heart of a place I love in ways words cannot; I am thankful for eyes to see his art.

Marlais Olmstead Brand
2015